# Eating with Veterans

## Michael Lund

BeachhouseBooks

Saint Charles  Missouri  USA

Copyright © 2015 Michael Lund

Eating with Veterans

Cover design by John Lund

ISBN 978-1-59630-100-9

LCCN 2015946173

BeachHouse Books

www.beachhousebooks.com

an Imprint of
Science & Humanities Press
Saint Charles MO 63301
(636) 394-4950

# Permissions

Some of the stories in this volume have been previously published in slightly altered forms: "Stratego" first appeared in *War Stories: Veterans Short Stories* (MilSpeak Books, 2012); "Drugs Away" in *Blue Falcon Review: A Journal of Military Fiction* Volume 1, (2013); "The Soy Bean Field" in *Outside-In Literary and Travel Magazine*, Issue Fifteen (Fall, 2013); "The Death of Short-timer Sam" in *Anak Sastra: Stories for Southeast Asia*, Issue Fourteen (January 2014); "Blood Drive" in *Beatdom* # 15 (July, 2014); and "Hadrian's Wall" in the *Veterans Writing Project Review* (Summer 2014 Volume 2 Number 4. We are grateful for permission to reprint these stories here.

Images and quotes within this book that are excerpted in brief form are used in accordance with fair use interpretation of U.S. Copyright Law and the Digital Millennial Copyright Act. Every attempt has been made to attribute and credit excerpted material correctly. Any errors or omissions should be brought to the attention of the publisher and will be corrected in future editions of the book. This work of fiction represents only the writer's opinions, ideas, and imagination, and not those of any other organization, institution, or person.

# Acknowledgements

During the time I was composing these stories many friends, some veterans some not, graciously let me speak about my experiences. All these individuals have responded in various ways to what I have to say, leading to many improvements in this volume. There is not space to list all, but the following deserve special mention: Allen and Donna Breckenridge, Bill and Angie Frank, Elizabeth Magill, Willie Smith, Bob and Ruth Partlow, John Miller, Ramon and Phyllis Stafford, Geoff and Kathy Orth, Bernard Edelman, Eldon Winslow, Roy and Prudence Reed, Carleton Davenport, Jennifer Gallagher Jones, and, of course, Anne Lund.

The cover was designed by my son, John, who, like his sister Meredith, carries on the fine tradition of dining and sharing stories. In addition to proofreading the manuscript, Beckie Smith offered especially wise suggestions for the final revision.

My gratitude to my publisher, Dr. Bud Banis, is unrestrained and enduring. His selfless dedication in bringing to many different audiences books he feels have merit ought to inspire others in an often market-driven industry. Science and Humanities Press is innovative in publishing, traditional in content, inspiring in purpose.

# Preface: Eating with Veterans

Only when I had finished a good draft of most of these stories did I realize the characters were often seen eating—eating and talking. I realized then that this was no accident, as most of these characters are aging veterans who look for places to voice their thoughts. And throughout all ages and in all cultures, sharing a meal allows us to put into words what we have experienced. When wine is added, of course, tongues are even looser.

In these pages, then, sometimes older vets eat with younger ones; on other occasions they share a table with civilians; a few times they are a group by themselves. Their mealtime companions can be family, friends, acquaintances, even relative strangers; but inevitably in the course of conversation some aspect of their military experience surfaces. Many times what is revealed has been long concealed, though only in a few cases could such moments be classified as what is termed in one story "the F-word," a flashback to a traumatic event. Still, when finally in the open, the remembered experience puts into perspective the lives and values of all who are present.

So, this volume of stories is an event to which I invite readers of all kinds. Partake of those tales that appeal to you. Put aside any that don't suit your tastes. My hope is a few will inspire memory, thought, and a desire to respond in word or deed. In an era when only a small percentage of citizens choose to serve in the military, the stories of those who do deserve at least the attention of the rest of us.

# Table of Contents

# The Rules of Engagement

"Another school shooting," observed Jackson, lowering the latest front page of the *Richmond Times Dispatch* and shaking his head. "This time near Boston. Seems like there's one every other day."

There was a murmur of understanding in the group of mostly retirees (male except for Parks and Samantha) enjoying coffee at McDonalds. Wilson, who characterized himself as "a contrarian," commented, "One *every* day, if you ask me." He had been studying the business section.

Some eyes rolled, and then Vandermill wondered, "Is there anywhere safe now? America has changed, my friends, in our lifetimes. Everyone has a gun, and everyone else is a potential target."

"I have to reject the black and white nature of your assertions," said Gene. "Besides, I know it's still safe at the best car dealership in America."

There were groans all around, and Samantha stood. Having heard Gene tout Harmon Motors in Amelia, a little town twenty-five miles to the east, as the best in the country many times, she didn't want him to derail the conversation about gun violence. She had her own ideas about the apparent nationwide epidemic of random shootings.

"Refills?" she asked. All hands rose, including Gene's, so she scooped up the Monopoly dice and went to the counter. The coffee crowd was an informal spin-off of the local VFW. Members ranged from the World War II era (Jackson) through Korea (Vandermill) to several who served in Iraq (Parks, Miller) and Afghanistan (Samantha). The others had been in Vietnam.

Vandermill put down the sports page and shook his head. "The topic is violence in America, Gene, not businesses. I'm pretty sure Amelia County has as many hunters with rifles as Piedmont County. And others keep handguns by their beds as a matter of principle. So, if it hasn't happened there yet, it's going to one day. We need to ask why."

Gene shrugged. "All I'm saying is that when a man walked into Harmon's waving a 45 and saying he was going to slaughter every man, woman, and child in the place, not a person was hurt."

"Whoa!" objected Wilson. "When did we declare this Tall Tales Day? Somebody get the hook."

The retired veterinarian was often a danger to the group conversation's forward motion. He could explode with a parliamentarian's zeal about rules of order, and they would soon be lost in deliberation of who could speak next and on what subject.

As he did frequently, Gene leapfrogged the potential roadblock. "I'm not making this up, my friends. Of course," he noted, "you already have proof it didn't play out the way the man predicted: here I am alive and well to tell you about it."

Samantha, the classified section of the paper folded under one arm, returned with a tray full of coffee refills and a dozen individual fruit pies. "Okay, guys, dig in." No one had specifically ordered the two-for-a-dollar pastries, but she had made a good guess about how many were needed, even the division between cherry and apple. The number of sugars and creamers was also accurate.

"Turn in the dice, Sam" said Vandermill, gesturing to the middle of the table. Whoever ended up with the Monopoly game pieces at the end of the day would take orders and deliver tomorrow. The task rotated in a haphazard way around the group, depending on who would be there the next day. Now and then a review for fairness had to be conducted, but, by and large, the system worked equitably.

Jackson's curiosity was raised. "Okay, Professor, explain why mad gunmen holster their weapons in your magical town. I wager we'll find that it was a special case and that things are much the same in that community as in Boston."

A Fairfield native and retired editor of the *Fairfield News*, Gene could take any offhand comment as a springboard to a lecture or what he liked to term "a focused discussion." He also possessed an exhaustive knowledge of local history. Hence his nickname of "The Professor."

"Let me start by reporting sadly that the guy was a Vietnam vet, fulfilling the stereotype." There was a knowing nodding of heads. "But the first

3

thing I thought of was the Lattimers. Remember them?"

This was a couple who ran a local souvenir/emporium/gift shop. A drunken plumber with a dishonorable discharge from the Army had entered Woodville's This, That, and T'Other two years ago and killed husband, wife, and one bystander. Didn't have any idea who they were, just taking out his frustration with bullets.

"Wasn't around here then," noted Parks. Then she added thoughtfully, "If someone—family member, friend, neighbor—had reported him as a menace, maybe it wouldn't might ever have happened."

"You see, that's the problem today," explained Gene. "We think we can quantify and label every citizen. With all the data collected, we run the numbers, predict events, forestall tragedy. But human beings don't behave like objects in a physics lesson—forces and trajectories, collisions and momentum. We need to accept blurred lines, variety of types, unpredictability."

Samantha disagreed. "No, we need better equipment, improved surveillance, strong local government. You're living in a land of small-town myth from the last century." Her views, like those of the others, reflected not only her age but also her particular experience in the military.

Vandermill apparently wanted to forestall the continuation of an old debate between Samantha and Gene. "But now," he said to Gene, "get to the

4

situation in Amelia."

"All right." He opened a box and took a bite of a cherry pie. "So, I took Margaret's minivan over there for a regular checkup and new tires. I knew it would take some time, and I settled myself on one of their sofas."

"Ah, yes," nodded Jackson with a knowing grin. "The undistinguished brown naugahyde furniture in an office that hasn't been redecorated in half a century."

They had heard Gene commend the current Harmon (Charles, son of Gregory, son of Harrison, who'd founded the company a century ago) for refusing to go the way of big city dealerships. He never built a spacious, glittery showroom or spread a vast inventory out on his lots; there was no army of tailored sales clerks or uniformed service personnel trained to recommend costly repairs over easy fixes; nor had he hired a big city marketing firm to send out surveys and construct advertising campaigns. The business relied almost entirely on word of mouth.

Gene went on. "Sitting there with the day's crossword, I watched a steady stream of customers come and go. They have a DMV in the same building, you know, so some folks are just getting renewal tags or changing plates. You can't tell when they come in."

Samantha, who'd heard his description of Harmon more than once, chimed in. "And the 'ladies' who do that work are all plainly dressed,

5

polite country women good at record keeping and smiling." She had objected before to the gender bias in staffing; the issue didn't seem important to Parks. Gene always insisted men applied only for the job of mechanic, women only for clerical positions. According to him, people were gravitating to their rightful places in an open field.

He ignored Samantha. "So, first off there was an elderly white man whose Chrysler 300 'engine repair' light popped on every few hundred miles for no reason. After listening to him patiently for fifteen minutes, James, the office manager—he's African-American you know—spun the computer around to show him an update on the problem. 'We can do the fix today if you have half an hour, or schedule you for later in the week."

"Get to the guy with the gun, please," said Vandermill, a CPA who had kept a handful of clients after retirement so he'd have a reason to come to the office for a few hours every day. "Or I'll have to ask you to give up the floor."

Gene ignored him also. "Then a young Asian woman with three children in tow—beats me why they weren't in school—comes in to say that every few days her rear PT Cruiser seat belts are yanked out of their clasps by the retractors. I thought right away the kids were rocketing themselves out of those restraints because one was already unpacking the new car brochures by the door, another had wandered around the corner to Charles's office, and the third plumped down beside me and whispered did I have any gum.

6

Jackson grunted. "They should have been taken to the woodshed. Kids today."

Gene smiled. "Clifford, the only other salesman at Harmon, herded them all up and took them out with him to inspect the car. Herded them all in again and told the lady they'd have to replace a couple of gizmos, could she bring it in Thursday or would she like to leave it and take a loaner, free of charge."

"Did she get the Grand Caravan?" mocked Wilson.

Gene smiled. "She did, indeed. Drove away thrilled, each child buckled in at a good distance from siblings."

Parks. "Then a guy with a gun walked in?"

"Nope. Half a dozen more people dropped off cars or picked them up in the next hour. Some paid in full; a few asked if they could wait until payday; others dug around in their overalls to come up with cash—I doubt it was enough in all cases. How James keeps track of who owes what is beyond me because he doesn't write down a thing."

"So, for some it's 'I'll pay you in chickens sort of thing'?" asked Jackson.

"'Barter' is a more sophisticated term. But, yes, not everything is done there by the books. Hey, I found out that there's a little Mexican grocery in Amelia now. Who'd have thought you'd be able get all sorts of authentic Hispanic foods and spices around here?"

Vandermill tried to get him back to the crisis situation. "So you're sitting there with the newspaper watching the comings and goings. You've given us the lead, how about 'the rest of the story'?"

Gene smiled. "I didn't have a notebook from my old reporting days out, but mentally I *do* keep track of who, what, where, when and why. But again, 'just the facts, ma'am' isn't always enough to figure out what's going on."

"If you don't get to the gunman, I'm going to …throw a pie at you," said Vandermill, looking around for a projectile to launch.

All these people had a high respect for the damage guns can do, having seen what is possible with sophisticated military hardware. They paid strict adherence to safety precautions themselves and, for the most part, avoided violence even in speech.

"Okay, okay. I'd been there about an hour and was wondering if I should step across the street to the diner for a cup of coffee—I missed you guys, see?"

The group assented to that logic.

"When this big guy—middle-aged, muscular, wearing all sorts of patriotic gear—pushed through the door gun in hand."

"Patriotic gear?"

"Flags sown into his jacket, stars and stripes on

8

pants, shoes, hat. There were slogans written all over his clothes, too, and he had tattoos in red, white, and blue."

"Someone off his meds, sounds like to me."

"A nut case, clearly. You take cover, Gene?"

"No time. And he was between me and the door. Not a happy situation, I assure you. I'd seen eyes like this before ...over there."

Again, the group nodded assent. Miller said, "Someone needed to take him out right there."

Samantha sighed. "Please, no one refer to the rules of engagement."

"In my day," said Jackson, "he's already dead."

Vandermill agreed.

"The world's gotten more complicated, that's for damn sure," shrugged Gene. "When can you fire? Anyway, there was no reason behind those eyes, just some blind fury. He didn't shout, but he had a huge voice—stentorious, he was. (I love to use that word, by the way.)"

Everyone knew not to rise to the bait—either why he liked it or exactly what it meant.

"So, the man proclaimed that America was headed to hell and he was going to put a stop to that, 'starting right here and now.' He pointed that 45 at the DMV lady, Alicia, who was frozen in her little window."

Everyone's coffee was empty, and the pies

were gone.

"I was mentally saying my farewells when Charles strolls out of his office. It's not much more than a closet, you know, off the waiting room."

"We know, we know. Get on with it."

"Yeah, still got that 1950s pine paneling on the walls—painted over in the '80s, though—the old wooden desk not right for the electronic equipment he has to keep in there, but he won't give it up. His daddy used to sit in the same spot, too. And you know, Gregory still comes in every day at age 91. 'Keeping my eye on the boy,' he says, pointing toward Charles, who's probably in his sixties."

"Right, right, third generation. Spent their whole lives in the county except when off in the military. They marry local girls, blah, blah, blah. What the hell happened? Pardon my language, ladies."

Samantha, ex-Marine, participated in the joke that they had to watch how they spoke around her. Former Air Force pilot Parks was somehow outside the issue.

"So Charles sees this guy and says, 'Willie, how you doing? Is your neighbor's old Aries holding up?' Walks right over to stand in front of him, between Willie and the DMV clerk. And the guy looks at him, not recognizing him, near as I can tell."

"Your chance to get away."

"I'm still in the guy's line of sight, three o'clock, and decide to stay still. Clifford comes out of the repair area and Charles turns to him. 'You know, it was this man's cousin, wasn't it, Cliff, the one who lived down off the main road south that we sold a truck to one time that he claimed could go faster in reverse than forward? Remember?"

"Cliff thought for a minute and said, 'That's right. Green Laramie SLT. Reliable as you'll find, though it did have its quirks."

"Charles turned to James, who'd been standing in his window the whole time. "That fella with the truck, he ever tell you about the Laramie going backwards so fast?' Still nothing from this Willie."

"James scratches his jaw a minute, then says, 'Tall guy, maybe six three, must have played some ball, if you ask me. Yeah, he did tell me about that truck. I told him, 'Bring it, man; we'll check it out.'"

Samantha offered. "But the dealer or someone had already pushed an alarm in his office, right, and they were just stalling until the police got there? Can't be far in that tiny town." She was an advocate of electronic security and top-notch communications systems.

"A block. But no; no alarm. Charles had just started chatting away the same way he does with anyone who comes in the shop or wanders by on the sidewalk. Asks them about their kin, neighbors, goings on in the community."

"Sort of like someone we know," laughed

Wilson. "A certain retired newspaper editor."

"Just like me, he was taught by his father, and he in turn by the grandfather. They know everyone and everything in that country stretching back into the century before the last. But Charles learned a lot more about people in his two Vietnam tours than I did. Even tried later to refine the ROEs but with little success."

"Tell me about it," muttered Samantha.

"So," prompted Vandermill, "Charles really did sell cars to the gunman's family?"

"Not a one. He was flying by the seat of his pants that day, saying whatever seemed right for the moment—or so it seemed anyway. Had no idea who this was—at least at first—but read his name printed over the shirt pocket, like on an Army uniform. Willie's kin, it turns out, are nearly all gone from around there, and when they were alive they got their cars in—something like what we described earlier—an informal kind of barter system."

"So this guy was local? Some people knew who he was?"

"Not really. We only learned later that he'd grown up in the county. We couldn't remember him exactly, even after he bought a car."

Vandermill shook his head. "Bought a car? You said you saw his eyes."

"Yeah, but Charles saw something else. The

way he held himself, for instance. He must have sensed a family resemblance, not to an individual but to all the men he was related to. And the stories Charles was telling borrowed from men like him, maybe even actual cousins or uncles or grandparents."

Wilson protested, "I'm still not understanding why the guy didn't open up on everyone. Not that I wouldn't want you here telling tales and picking up the dice for tomorrow. Everybody else coming?"

Again, assent.

Gene scooped up the dice from the center of the table and continued. "You see, in his chatter Charles drew Willie into the community, gave him a place, a set of connections. He suggested his kin were Amelia county natives, part of local history. And Charles' assertions were close enough to what was true—or to what Willie might have liked to believe—that he started nodding. It was as if he was remembering those experiences, maybe reliving them in his mind."

"Huh," offered Wilson. "Sort of like a spider weaving a web around a fly. When he got Willie all tied up, he turned him over to the authorities."

"After a bit, as he was listening to Charles, Willie tucked his gun into his belt. He leaned in, muttering 'Yeah, that's so,' or 'Now, I'd forgotten about that,' and 'Well, don't that beat all.' At one point he offered, 'Now, I remember that a bit differently. Wasn't a black bear, turns out, but a big black dog, dangerous, too, though in his own

13

way.'"

"By now several repairmen—oops! repair *persons*—had bought worksheets up to James, and he'd gone to totaling up bills. Clifford asked Alicia if those new DMV forms had come in. And Charles got around to mentioning he had some fine used cars out back, if Willie'd like to take a look. 'Seems to me you'd fit right in the Dodge Charger I've got. It has some miles on it, but runs real smooth.'"

Samantha puzzled. "That's it? Walked out back. What did the rest of you do?"

"Me? Well, James told me Margaret's car was ready, so I stepped up to pay the bill."

"How much was it, by the way—tires and all?"

"Don't have any idea. I just give James my credit card, and he rings it up."

"Geez! That's no way to run a business. But the guy's gun, Willie's, it was loaded? He drive off with it stashed in the Dodge Charger's glove compartment?"

"It was loaded, but he gave it to Charles. Asked him to put it in the office safe where nobody who shouldn't be handling a gun could get to it."

"Like a child …or a crazy person! So, he took off? Where'd he go?"

"Well, he and Charles settled on the price for the car, and when I left he was getting the license all straight."

14

"What did he have? A wad of bills stuffed in his pocket?"

"Not right then, but Charles figured he'd be able to pay once he got on the payroll."

"Oh, yeah, he got a job. Of course! Why didn't I see that coming?"

"Charles found out Willie'd had experience in the motor pool, could work on trucks and older model cars."

"So, now there's a mechanic working at Harmon's who should be in jail. Another reason to stay away from 'the best car dealership in America.'"

Gene pulled his coat off the back of the booth and rose. "Well, he'd be behind bars in Boston, I admit that. Wilson, you do the crossword?"

"Uh, no. You got us all sidetracked today—again. Take it." He tossed the entertainment section on the counter. "Hey, tomorrow, get us some of those cinnamon rolls, will you? We haven't had any in a while, and I got me a hunger for one."

"Can do. Just don't ask for the hash browns. There's too much grease in those things, and I worry about the health of you guys. I want us all to live a long and comfortable life."

He squinted out the window as if trying to remember where he'd parked his car. "It *can* be a dangerous world out there," he concluded. "So, be safe, my friends."

15

# Fire

Although she rarely used them, Jennifer had all the standard four-letter words in her vocabulary. She seldom wore provocative clothes, but she was—and was aware that she was— strikingly beautiful. Skillful at avoiding confrontation, she knew when not to back down. She thought of herself as a Midwesterner of the old school.

Whenever she narrated her and her husband Phil's experience in the upscale Boston restaurant, she remained calm and did not use what she referred to as "the F-word." The inept server, the spilled glass of wine, even the firefighters in full gear had not triggered an explosion from her or her husband; but when Philip Woods saw a woman squatting to examine something on the sidewalk, Jenny worried he was about to loose it ...and she him.

The F-word was appropriate to what followed, but it was also, she knew, a simplification, one label that covered too broad a spectrum of behavior. And she refused to package her husband's past in a term that was so little understood by the civilian population. She prayed she would not have to take action in front of a couple who had no idea he was reliving his time in Vietnam.

Over the years she had learned what to do

when an episode began: throw her arms around him and call, "Come here; come to *me*!" She knew he was rising out of a dream — or a nightmare — and regaining consciousness of his current surroundings; but she liked the idea he was also coming to terms with the past and joining her in the present. She believed that it worked because her love for him was so strong and because her faith had endured so many trials.

The Woods were celebrating their 35th anniversary by walking the Freedom Trail in "The Cradle of Liberty" and spending several nights on Cape Cod. For many years content to visit local landmarks (the St. Louis Arch, Meramec Caverns, Truman's home), they decided it would be educational to expand their horizons.

Their guides for this day's excursion were Marlene, a classmate of Jennifer's at Westminster thirty years ago, and her third husband, Lawrence. After touring Boston Common, the Old North Church, and Paul Revere's House, they chose the Thai Pepper Restaurant for dinner, located on the ground floor of the small but elegant Bright Hotel.

"You do like spicy food, don't you?" said Marlene cheerily. Neither of the Woods did.

"Sure," Jenny beamed, hopeful that she could read the menu well enough to avoid the hottest dishes. "My only culinary rule is that I don't want what I'm about to eat to still be moving." She deliberately didn't look at Phil, who would later pretend to be angry. He preferred simple, home-cooked meals.

"Oh, I know what you mean! One time in Seoul, I was served sannakji, baby octopus, still squirming on the plate ..." Marlene launched into a lengthy account of a feast given to her as CEO of Eagle, Inc., a global souvenir business that shipped American knickknacks to over forty countries.

Coming into the Thai Pepper, Jennifer saw that a boisterous party of eight had pushed two tables together and must have been into their second round of drinks; but it was early and the rest of the restaurant was empty. It would be a good place to continue their conversation. She believed that learning how others in your generation had fared allowed you to put your own life in perspective, especially when approaching retirement.

Marlene and Larry sat against the restaurant's far wall in order—they claimed conspiratorially— to study the sophisticated clientele who would begin drifting in before long.

"Ah," observed Phil, "but we can see, too." He glanced over the Royals' heads to the mirror behind them, which ran the length of the wall and in which he and Jennifer could view the entire setting. The other couple looked over their shoulders, nodded, then turned back to study the menus.

"This is on us, you understand," Marlene insisted. "You come to Boston once in thirty years, we insist on treating."

"You're too kind," said Jenny as the

conspicuously young-looking server approached. "But do let us get the tip."

It must have been the first night for poor Jeremy. Even his assertion that he would be "taking care of them" made Phil whisper it might end up the other way around. In fact, the young man would have to ask if the restaurant served Bombay gin, what white wine was recommended with the fish, if there was a dark beer on draft. Jenny was sympathetic, but Marlene made it clear, if he couldn't do any better than what she was seeing, this would be the end of a very short career.

Changing the topic, Phil asked, "Do you both travel a lot with your business?" He was also remembering vaguely what Jenny had told him about Marlene Bernstein's remarkable successes, reported more than once in the alumni magazine. She ran a small firm that had realized early the potential of the web to take clever ads viral.

"I go with Marlene anywhere they speak English," Larry grinned. "Of course, she gets to travel first class, and I'm used to that." He'd played varsity tennis for the University of Pennsylvania and was now a part-time teaching pro at the Cloisters, a small country club in Back Bay. "You guys?"

"That's something we're putting off until retirement, I guess." Jenny patted her husband on the arm, "Larry did his traveling before I met him."

"Ah," Marlene nodded, but Jenny wasn't at all sure her friend remembered Phil had served two tours in Southeast Asia.

Larry tilted his head to one side. "I feel like we're spying on passersby over there." The ground floor of the hotel was below street level, and a row of small windows just beneath the ceiling of the street-side wall showed pedestrians from their feet up to mid-thigh. "We can see them, but they can't see us."

"Are you looking up skirts again?" teased Marlene, though Jennifer felt her voice had an edge. The women striding by in high heels and short skirts were attractive, perhaps on their way home at the end of a long day. The men, too, mostly in suits, moved purposely, in some cases the bottoms of their briefcases swinging forward just below the top of the windows.

"*There's* the skirt to look up," said Jenny, lowering her voice. She raised her eyes in the mirror to direct their attention. "Well, it would be if she were wearing one."

A slender young woman in a cerise pink blouse and sleek black slacks was gliding in, ushered to a table by their awkward server. The woman's escort looked as if he had just come from skippering an America's Cup yacht, beige sweater tied around his neck over a light blue shirt. He wore white linen slacks.

"The upper crust," whispered Phil, acknowledging the couple's easy aristocratic manner.

20

Jenny was happy that his attention had been diverted from the street scene. One of the triggers for his episodes seemed to be connected to a woman kneeling or squatting, her legs folded beneath her.

"I've never been able to look that comfortable," complained Marlene, signaling the server with a raised finger. She thought her martini not dry enough and asked for another.

"I've always said you have to be born to money to be that easy in your skin," observed Larry, who, coming from an old Brahmin family, proved his own point. Marlene had clawed her way to the top from a middle-class Nebraska background; and all the coaching she had had could not give her the air of being to the manor born.

Phil ran a finger through the moisture on his beer mug. "Class gets you in the door, but after that you have to be able to do the job." He had started his own insurance company after four years in the military and then college. His recruiting had proven he was a good judge of character. Over the years, he turned down opportunities to expand or create satellite offices; he and Jenny enjoyed their small-town life in northeastern Missouri. They both had family in the area.

"So, how far away *is* retirement?" Marlene asked, when the salads arrived. "I'm not sure I can give up jetting around the world and seeing, you know, the Great Wall of China, the Taj Mahal, lions and elephants in Africa."

Jenny paused, realizing the house's chili dressing must have taken the place of the walnut vinaigrette she had ordered. "We wouldn't mind spending some time out west—Yellowstone, Glacier, the Grand Tetons. Phil likes cool climates and open vistas."

They all looked up at the sound of something falling, broken glass. At first they assumed the party of eight had caused the disturbance; and Jenny worried that the candles on their tables had crashed onto the floor. But that crowd, too, was looking around for the source of the noise. In the mirror, Jenny saw the young aristocratic woman in pink silk standing back from her chair and brushing the front of her blouse and pants.

"Oh my God!" said Marlene. "That idiot dropped a glass of red wine on her. Well, he's toast for sure."

They all watched as the manager raced out, full of apologies, bowing and wringing his hands. He took several napkins from a neighboring table and offered them to the couple. Jenny could hear him say he would pay to have her clothes cleaned and that dinner was on the house.

Phil leaned forward and said, "Can you believe this? She's sitting back down! They're going to stay and eat."

In fact, the young woman was as relaxed as before, smiling at the unfortunate event as if it could have happened to anyone, as if no real harm had been done. Her companion smiled, too, as he

22

sipped his wine, completely focused, for all they could tell, on what she was saying.

Jenny said, "Maybe it mostly missed her. She did seem to be mopping the table and the chair. Still, they're both pretty cool."

"Hell," Marlene said, "she probably has a dozen outfits back in her penthouse. Or Mr. Preppie will buy her one after dinner."

"In order to have her take it off before the night is over," added Larry with a wink.

Jenny imagined the young couple to be passionate, but deliberate; energetic but sensitive; polished. It was not clothes that made them attractive. Slim and fit, they had the grace of dancers and could have made bargain wardrobes inconspicuous in a celebrity fashion show.

The food at the Thai Pepper was good, though spicy enough that the Woods ate slowly and drank extra water (pulling out the lemon slices). Their sad server put the dishes before the wrong people, forgot the bread, did not catch Phil's request for another beer. As the men ate quietly, the women chatted about classmates spread around the nation.

"You know what one of our biggest new sales item is?" Marlene asked, spearing her last piece of filet mignon. "Naughty tattoo kits."

"She's right," Larry agreed. "But you wouldn't know it from the catalog. The pictures show eagles, flags, cannons; but the tattoo sheets can be refolded to become a stripper with fans, legs entangled, a man's privates."

"How do your customers overseas know?" Phil asked.

"Oh, we have someone on the ground distributing a key to the catalog and some samples. Kids are ready to order before they learn how, and their parents think it's cute that they want to be American. Of course, they have to put the tattoos where only their close friends can see them."

"'We fill their jeans'," laughed Marlene, alluding to what must have been a company slogan, "but also our pockets."

Looking up from the dessert menu, Larry's eyes widened and his mouth fell open.

"What?" asked Phil quietly.

"She's borrowed his sweater. And she's putting it on over her wet blouse."

Marlene, on her third martini, had lost interest; but Jenny and Phil watched discretely as the young woman under the too large man's sweater hitched a shoulder, tucked an arm up, twisted her torso. After a few moments, she pulled her blouse out from the bottom of the sweater and folded it neatly into her tiny black purse.

"How did she do that?" wondered Jennifer. "Were their buttons? I guess there weren't. Still ..."

"Oh, Lord, tell me her bra is wet, too," implored Larry.

24

There was one more round of discrete wiggling, but then the young woman settled down.

Phil laughed. "There was no bra in there, Larry. Her breasts are too firm to need one."

Jenny slapped him playfully on the hand.

"Hot, hot, hot!" insisted Larry.

Marlene said, "I hope we're *not* going to be hot! Look." She was pointing to the windows that revealed the sidewalk. The high boots of firefighters had appeared, canvas hoses, a double-edged axe balanced in a gloved hand.

"They're not racing around, though" observed Phil. "Mostly standing there. I wonder what's up."

"There's one, the captain, I think," said Larry, gesturing toward the entrance where a tall man was talking to the manager. He had on his helmet, the familiar heavy jacket, an oxygen mask and tank strapped to his back.

Jenny used the mirror to inspect Phil. There was something about fire that could trigger the bad memories. She didn't think it was like the famous napalm incident, the young Vietnamese girl, naked, running into the camera. But he didn't like fire, once breaking oddly into a detailed explanation of the Army's M2A1 flamethrower, used by both American and South Vietnamese soldiers. His face was flushed.

"Phil, honey," she asked, shaking his elbow to rouse him. "Could you …ah, go ask Jeremy what's going on out there?"

She hoped making him stand up and look elsewhere might help. Too, because he felt sorry for the unfortunate, he would probably see it as a chance to make Jeremy more relaxed. Focusing on that goal might make him flash forward.

Phil's episodes had come more frequently in the last few years, perhaps because the United States was back at war again—and again. He watched the news sparingly and was restless in his sleep. Having to work less hard at the office might also be giving his mind more time to roam over the past. Jenny wondered if he would have to resume the counseling that had been life-saving years ago. She had read that suicide rates among veterans went up as they aged and as both physical and mental conditions worsened.

"You know what I never got used to?" he'd asked her recently, out of the blue. "Poor women, refugees, squatting beside the road to …to do their business."

"I assume there were no public toilets available," Jennifer said sadly.

"No, of course not. But, really, it's not so different from what you do when camping, except that it's public. They look so vulnerable …in that position. Of course, some of the women we saw turned out to be VC, female soldiers."

Phil came back to the table, bringing the young server with him. "Jeremy's found out—false alarm.

Someone in one of the rooms upstairs thought he smelled smoke. The trucks are required to come if an alarm is triggered." From the blank look on the boy's face, Jenny knew Phil was giving him credit for the discovery he had made himself.

They all turned to the windows to watch the firefighters pulling in the hoses, pedestrians making room for their work. A woman in heels stopped for a moment as a hose coiled across her path. When she knelt to pick up something from the sidewalk, they could see it was the same elegant young woman who had been doused by wine, a strand of hair falling across her face as she bent down. She and her companion must have slipped out while the two couples were eating dessert. One knee nearly came down on the sidewalk while the other pointed up, her black pants leg pulled along her calf.

"Oh, here we go: looking up skirts again," said Marlene. Examining the check closely, she declared. "Fuck! He's overcharged us."

The woman outside had turned toward the window and hunkered down in what seemed to be an uncomfortable position. Jenny wondered if she had lost the back of an earring. Or was she peering through the window at them?

"Look out!" said Phil, so loudly that even the table of eight looked in his direction. Only Jenny, who followed his gaze, understood the significance of the fire extinguisher nozzle and hose arcing toward the squatting woman's head.

As if she had heard Phil, though, the woman outside turned her head, saw the threat just in time, and — throwing one arm up — ducked further down. Her dinner companion knelt beside her, his arm protectively coming across her shoulder; and the fire extinguisher was pulled back by a gloved hand. Accident averted!

Jennifer felt an explosion had been averted inside the restaurant as well. Copying the man on the sidewalk, Phil had instinctively put his arm around her. She tilted her head to his ear and whispered, "Come here; come to *me*!"

He squeezed her shoulder and coughed nervously. Then he told the others, "Sorry about yelling out there. I thought she was going to get ...clobbered." They understood. And they laughed at the evening's series of odd events.

Jenny knew they would recount the zany dinner in Boston many times to their friends back in the Midwest. But she didn't think she and Phil would want a repeat date with Marlene and Larry.

That night, back in their cottage at Cape Cod, naked in bed, Jennifer studied Phil's hand as he lay asleep beside her. She knew a lot of words that could be used to describe her husband, herself, their marriage. The four-letter one that mattered was "here."

# Drugs Away

That Charlie got his brains spread over the Cambodian treetops made most of them forget that he'd been the chief scriptwriter for a doomed radio propaganda series. "Insane," he'd called *Drugs Away;* but the rest of them came to realize he was the crazy one. Still, maybe he'd been a genius, after all. "Sad loss," they told others back home, privately including themselves among the casualties.

The radio serial, to be broadcast in-country, was the brainchild of "Mad" Major Moon, who saw it as an effective anti-drug tool. His previous assignment had been near Chicago, where he was addicted to WCFL's *Chicken Man*. That ongoing comic drama of a would-be super hero originated in the Windy City and was then syndicated on, among other places, Armed Forces Radio.

"We'll call our show *Drugs Away*," the major told his soldiers. "You know, like 'Bombs Away.' The hero is named Smash. Sidearm is his diminutive sidekick."

*"Turds Away,"* whispered Charlie to Mark, one of the other information specialists Mad Moon assigned to the project. Aloud he said, "You wouldn't want to go with something more conventional, sir, akin to 'Waste Water Means Water Shortage?'"

29

Mark, like Charlie a fellow former DJ, added, "Hmm. Yes. 'Pot Lips Send Smoke Signals'? That's catchy."

Gerry, the third man on the team, was sleeping on the floor of the sound booth, and both Charlie and Mark hoped he was drunk enough not to wake until Mad Moon left. Gerry, though, would be the first to see how *Drugs Away* drew out Charlie's weakness as well as his strengths.

"We're going to have drama, men," Major Moon insisted. "Add some fire to the campaign!"

Mark asked, "Okay sir, what happens in each episode. Does Smash go after the bad guys?"

"Of course, private. But he never catches the big boys, know what I mean? Potter, the most dastardly dealer in all of Gotham." The men would later call him "Putter," "Butter," "Pothole," "Butthole."

"Ah," Charlie chimed in. "So, listeners tune in for more episodes, hoping the villain is finally apprehended ...or exploded, or drowned in a wooden barrel of oil, or incinerated in a tower of flame?"

Mark's eyes widened. He recalled how Charlie, on night guard duty, was fascinated by the Cobra gunships "working out," as they said, on suspected enemy units. The minigun's lines of fire were, he said with genuine admiration, "fucking lasers!"

"Good, sir," said Mark to Major Moon. "But,

30

um, there needs to be some sort of climax to each show, doesn't there? I mean, I'm sure you've thought of that."

Mad Moon eyed him suspiciously. He worried that the draftees in this unit, most of whom had more education than he did, were mocking him. "Hell yes, I've thought of that. Smash and Sidearm find a group of users and their equipment each time, see. And what happens is, they crash into a house—or a tent, or a Quonset hut—and they kick the shit out of everything—the pipes, the syringes, all that …that …paraphernalia. Smash lights into it screaming 'Drugs Away!' and the lowlife yell, faint, run for their lives."

"I can see that happening," agreed Mark, deliberately not exchanging glances with Charlie.

"We can give you noise," added Charlie, convincingly. "Smash will fucking explode! Excuse me, sir." He ducked his head, as if he'd spoken inappropriately. "I mean, he'll blow things up, sir."

"That's okay, Specialist. And you're damn right he will."

So the project began, despite the enlisted men's conviction that such a program would never be aired. They could script episodes, record and edit them; but there was no chance in hell, they believed, that the top brass would let them be broadcast.

"It's announcing to everyone that we know there's a drug problem in Vietnam, for Christ's

31

sake," explained Gerry later. A genius in his own way, he had concocted a scheme that let him work on his own schedule even in a war. "We've made a major effort to cover it up for months. Now we're going to confirm what the mainstream media has been reporting? Nevah happen, G.I."

The Information Office's mission, of course, was to control the story. By this point, coverage of the protest movement was extensive back home, and the in-country correspondents seemed interested only in tales of waste, ineffectiveness, low morale, drug use. Once hungry for genuine news of military progress, they were now on an anti-war feeding frenzy.

"Still," Charlie winked, "I smell a good gig here." He rose to an exaggerated position of attention. "From this day forward, men, we're busy …hell, we're enamored, possessed, enraptured by the *Drugs Away* project. We can't go out on other stories or bother ourselves with routine jobs 'cause this baby is going to consume us."

Mark later remembered the word "consume" as prophetic. But at the time he grinned and snapped off a salute. "Right you are, *sir*! It's a damned creative challenge to come up with great ideas, so it's going to take time, energy, in-ten-si-*ty*!" He paused conspiratorially.

"But we *are* writers! We've just got to isolate the team from the everyday, the hoi polloi, the this and that. We'll brainstorm, feed off each other's genius to make this the best goddamned radio show Vietnam has ever seen …well, heard." He didn't realize that *Drugs Away* would feed on them all, but especially on Charlie, who was drawn by more than the creative challenge. Without realizing it, he was crossing the line between reality and fantasy.

Still, the great boondoggle of their tour had begun. And it was not one they had dreamed up themselves, but one they'd been assigned. Fortunately, they were able to keep what they were doing hidden from the civilian press, who would have gone wild with the story.

Charlie explained the *Drugs Away* scheme to his new friends at the enlisted men's club, three veterans finishing the last weeks of their tour after experiences in the field they would not discuss. Jimmy, an infantry platoon leader, was not surprised that the Army was putting men to work on such a project. "There it is," he said, lighting another Marlboro. "Another reason to keep officers in the rear."

"Now, now. Some of those USARV-HQ colonels are falling all over each other to get out in the field," said Wayne. The former adviser to an ARVN unit was half right, of course: promotion came with combat experience. And some officers, they admitted, were truly motivated, gung-ho to be with the men. Nearly all the enlisted men in USARV-HQ, however, were happy to be in so well fortified a base that they could enjoy bowling lanes, swimming pools, restaurants, and well-stocked PX's. Their worst enemy was boredom.

"I've taken my share of them into battle," said Skyking, a chopper pilot. "Wait! Make that '*over* battle'; i.e. a few thousand feet above the action where I could keep them safe." The name "Prince" was printed on his uniform; but, out of the bush, he promoted himself to the next rank. He was the guy who would get Charlie on the bird that was shot out of the air over Memot, in Cambodia.

"I've been on a night ambush," Charlie boasted. "Wanted to record the sound, you know — the jungle quiet, the nocturnal animals, wind in the reeds. Then, blam, rat-a-tat-tat, kablooee! Blown to smithereens. I had three different recorders set up." He sighed. "But nothing happened."

Jimmy knew the lieutenant who'd led the patrol. When his CO said he had to take the 71R with him, he set up where the Viet Cong were least likely to be. He didn't want this asshole's death on his conscious. He had enough of them already.

Wayne announced, "Another round," not a question but an assertion. The issue was who would pay. Wayne had a nervous tic, the left side of his face flinching randomly. It wasn't clear why he hadn't been put on a Freedom Bird going home yet.

He and the others, though, were willing to hear Charlie's ideas for *Drugs Away*, a goofy distraction from whatever they thought about when they were alone. Immune to the seductive charm of comic book heroism, they would still chime in with suggestions, like Jimmy's proposed chicken coop/chicken poop scenario.

It was inspired by Charlie's mock daily news feed: "A chicken coop was broken into south of Dung Heap yesterday," he would intone in his deepest announcer voice, entertaining visitors from other offices. "Fifteen hundred enemy were killed. There were no friendly casualties, though one CO got egg on his face and one hen was …well, we'd better not go into what happened to her."

"So, you've got a bunch of guys smoking pot in a Vietnamese chicken coop, see," explained Jimmy. "They're passing around a pipe, and then it runs out. So, one guy …"

"PFC Shitforbrains," offers Skyking.

" …PFC Shitforbrains looks for the stash in and amongst—you can use that word, *amongst*—the nests."

"And he finds a pile of dried chicken shit!" laughs Charlie. "They're smoking it up, and Smash crashes in, tears the place apart, but Sidearm can't find the weed. Busted!"

They cleaned the script up, of course, and there was pot in the coop. They titled it "Chicken Feed," and every time the phrase was used they drew it out and inserted a long pause in the middle: "chickennnnn …*feed*!" Major Moon loved the echo of Chicken Man.

The only problem was figuring out how to make the sound of nests being ripped apart. Breaking eggs was easy—real eggs from the mess hall. Finally they decided rustling papers was close enough. The old saw about making an omelet was told too many times, however.

Meanwhile Charlie was trying to get the grunts to talk about what they'd seen. "It was bad out there, huh?" he'd say to Wayne, who would have his back to the band from the Philippines playing on stage, three women gyrating to classic American rock-n-roll, a male drummer.

He responded, "It's bad everywhere, man."

"How about you, Sky? Were you able to stay above it all, so to speak, or did you get down into the shit?"

"We all get into it sooner or later. Ain't that right, Jimmy?"

"So they tell me."

Charlie's attention switched to the lead dancer, whose steps resembled a stripper's, though no clothes came off. Her bump and grind took her in a complete circle, her ass a rotating miracle. The other three seemed to have no interest in the music or the girl. Each night they drank steadily until the club closed, their expressions unchanging except for Wayne's recurring tic.

Charlie told a long tale about flying on a Medevac chopper, wanting to make an audio feature about rescue operations. In a rare moment of restraint, Mad Moon nixed the project when he was told how many times that story had been done.

The goal of some enlisted journalists was to get out of the office for a week or two, supposedly in search of Vietnamization success stories. Nixon, frantic about the upcoming election, was demanding they produce evidence that the host country was taking on responsibility for its own survival. Reporters were careful to manage only one short feature for each trip, though, so the officers wouldn't expect much from their comrades. Polishing each story could take a week or more.

Gerry had done one better. While assigned to audio, he was also a good photographer and took pictures wherever he went. Since the dark room belonged to the official photographers, he could only develop and print at night. After a while, he also began to work in the radio studio then as well.

One top sergeant left and a new one came, unfamiliar with the routine. Mark explained that Gerry worked the night shift, as if it were an established practice. And so it was for the rest of Gerry's tour.

*Drugs Away*, though, was the perfect project to fill the days for Charlie, Mark and Gerry as they concocted plots, reworked them, recorded a couple of proposed pilot episodes. They loved to add new sounds to the climactic scenes: rocks rattling inside a helmet, fists pounding sandbags, whiskey bottles broken into a fifty-gallon barrel.

There were also screams, cries, yips, and barks as Smash ran, leaped, dropped on top of offenders. Men from photojournalism, *Stars and Stripes*, daily releases were eager to help, adding new voices, moans and groans, the pleas of surrender. The recording sessions were relief from tension and boredom. The project, a stretch to begin with, was spinning completely out of control.

The more episodes of *Drugs Away* Charlie wrote, the more bizarre the situations depicted. It was as if the author were coping with his own demons by vicariously exposing and rescuing fictional characters from tight spots. His creations would seek escape from the war on drugs but feel anxiety about getting caught, guilt for failing to be men. The tension would grow through the 30-minute plot to a point of unbearable intensity. Then, Smash flew onto the scene in a righteous rage, his anger an expression of everyone's vague frustrations.

Charlie was the voice of Smash. Gerry and Mark noted the manic tones in his performances. They tried, unsuccessfully, to get him to tone it down. "You ain't Smash, man. Or Chickenman. You're still a plain old troop."

In "Trash Can Can" half a dozen troops were smoking dope in a giant corrugated metal waste bin, with a lookout sending increasingly nervous alerts to the others. "I think I hear a noise, man." "We're goin' get busted. I feel it." "There's someone out there, I'm telling you."

Charlie wasn't content to have Smash and Sidearm swing open the metal door, arrest the men, and confiscate their paraphernalia. He wanted his super heroes to parachute in from above, screaming "Airborne! Drugs Awayyyyy!" They rubbed a green T-shirt to make the sound of a parachute and blew into the microphone for wind. Mad Moon told them to get cookie sheets from the mess hall, throw them into the wall, bounce them off metal chairs.

In the evenings, Charlie drank with his short-timer buddies, always trying to elicit their stories of combat. He also began to work on Skyking to get him a ride on a Cobra gunship. Their mini-guns fired one hundred rounds per second. "One hundred thrills a minute?" he asked Sky.

"You could say that."

"Did you ever take passengers, when things were quiet, I mean?"

"Fuckin' joy-riding officers."

"They loved it?"

"The lucky ones."

"I have a friend of a friend who owes me one, you know what I mean? And he can get anyone who'll take me up a thirty-minute MARS call back home. And, hell, I'll record the sounds of the flight, make it a great feature story."

The next *Drugs Away* scenario had men mainlining on a beach of the South China Sea. Mad Moon ironically got that script started. Irritated that his project was not being automatically endorsed at the next level of command, he insisted on spreading the show's range. "It's the units with cushy assignments on the coast that get away with shit," he explained. "We'll target their asses."

Charlie said, "Smash will come on them from out of the sea. He'll have his frogman suit, the snorkel, fins. He'll be like a typhoon, a waterspout, fuckin' Neptune firing lightning bolts from his hands and blasting everything with his trident. It'll be a spectacular episode!"

The Major stared at him for a moment, as if he sensed something more than the usual bitterness of draftees in Charlie's face. "Don't let it get too complicated, Troop. Just make it clear that drug use is hurting the mission and that we'll kick the ass of anyone we catch."

The enlisted men suspected the top brass were less concerned with what the grunts did than with how support troops in the rear got their recreation. Men in the field knew they couldn't all be high and survive. And controlled marijuana use may have helped them get through the dangers they faced and perform the inhuman acts required of the infantry.

"Hey, and give us a sighting of Potter this time," the Major added. "We've got to keep the theme going, that there's a super villain behind the scenes. He's got ties to the North, to China, to Communists back in the good old U. S. of A. Motherfuckin' peaceniks!"

So, Charlie went to work inserting Potter sightings into the next episode of *Drugs Away*—

piloting a fishing coracle, selling black market watches from a rickshaw, disguised as a water buffalo. At the same time, he didn't let up in his other campaign.

Sky must have tired of being bugged about a gunship ride, so he passed word on that a correspondent he knew wanted to do a story about chopper operations. Maybe strings were pulled, I.O.U.'s called in. It could all have been done on the sly, no one quite sure who authorized it.

But early one morning, Charlie hitched a ride over to Cu Chi, where he found a parking lot full of probably one hundred Cobras. Their blades folded, they resembled giant insects. Thinner than the Hueys or Chinooks, they looked as if they could slip into cracks or seams and open up the universe. One had a seat for him.

All the guys had seen Cobras at one time or another, hovering over enemy positions and sending down a stream of machine gun fire. Only one in five rounds was a tracer, but from a mile away it looked as if a line of light was unzipping the earth. The sound was more a hum than a series of pops. They also had rockets for larger targets.

The ships would rise up singly or in small groups from the air base, tip their noses toward the ground, and swing off on a mission. Charlie couldn't believe how many were on the airstrip, parked in orderly rows with busy crews getting them ready for action. The prospect took his breath away.

What brought down the one he was on no one could say, though it had strayed over the border, dangerous even after the Cambodian Incursion. Sky made the announcement and Jimmy the conclusion: "It don't mean nothin'."

The men in HQ-IO hid their fear in the usual clever phrases: Charlie, the creator of Smash (descendant of Chickenman), had donned his superhero outfit, flown after the bad guys, and turned himself into "ass ash," made "Smash hash," "crashed." Everybody marked off another day on their short-timer calendar.

At about the same time, the brass killed *Drugs Away*, exactly as predicted. Entertaining, but highlighting a problem better dealt with quietly.

After a period of anger, Mad Moon rebounded. He found a new obsession: stopping the flow of empty beer cans into the black market. They ended up hammered together into tin walls for refugee huts erected on the edges of towns. And he was sure they were housing sappers, spies, the enemy. Another team began researching *Beer Can Alley*.

When they got back to the World, though, Mark and Gerry exchanged a few letters about the tragedy. A great mind had been lost, perhaps a genius. They would get together themselves one day, the two of them, and produce a new radio feature in his honor. They were talented writers themselves who, taking a vacation together with their families in peacetime, could create a legend,

"The Father of Smash."

This time, though, it would be about a peacekeeper, someone who defused tension, resolved conflict. *War Away* or something like that, with a hero who calmed troubled waters. After dinner at a classy resort, drinking a fine wine as their wives put the children to bed, they would write the story for their buddies, those who came home. And it would be a tribute to all who had been injured, embodied in tales of the zany wild man whose gift for words and story was unique.

They didn't do it, of course, more ready than they knew to leave it all in the past. The present was now, and who would really care, anyway?

# Holy Grass

I.

At 2:00 in the morning, as Hurricane Iris was tearing into Hartford, Edward Winston, aged 91, drove himself to the Rescue Squad station. He worried that he might be having a heart attack.

"Why didn't he call 9/11 or someone — like his daughter?" Curtis later asked his neighbor, Martha Anne. He'd driven down two days after the storm to see about the retirement house he and Elizabeth were restoring. Now the son was shining, but hard-at-work chain saws and a wood chipper were making it hard for him to hear.

"Oh, that's Ed! He knew they'd turn on the siren, and he didn't want everyone to get worried about him. Even with all he's been through, he insists on taking care of himself." Edward's house was at the end of the block by the drawbridge. To get there an ambulance would have to drive through the center of town, all of a block long. The wail would wake everybody.

Curt knew Edward had lost his wife a few years ago, before he and Beth bought the Newton House; but the way Martha Anne spoke, he sensed there was something else in his neighbor's past she was not mentioning.

"So," he asked, still not believing, "the wind

44

howling, rain flying parallel to the ground, water crashing over bulkheads, power out, he got in his pick-up and drove across town?"

"Yes," chuckled Martha Anne. "And he found the Rescue Squad asleep! He had to wake them up and get them to check his pulse, his breathing, his blood pressure."

"I'm surprised he didn't decide to go back to work for them right then and there!" After he retired from the post office, Edward had been a volunteer for over twenty years. "But you say he's all right—that's good. Say, did you stay here also?"

Curtis had sat out one hurricane himself in the old two-story frame house he and his wife had purchased five years earlier. The wind blew so hard the tin roof buckled and popped like cannon fire, rain rattled the windows, loose in their casements, and the sound of limbs being ripped off giant cypresses and slamming to the ground had made him vow never to stay for another.

"Oh, yes. Being on this side of Front Street makes a big difference. Your side looses dirt in the storm surge and takes the worst of the wind. I'd bought supplies, filled the bathtub, had the kerosene lamps ready." She turned back to picking up sticks and stacking them beside the street, remarkably mobile for her 86 years. "Anyway, the Rescue Squad decided Ed had just had a bit of an anxiety attack. Now he's back working in his garden."

"The garden from which he gives away 90% of

45

what he grows!"

"You'll be doing the same with your new garden, too, one day. You're a lot like him."

Martha Anne's matter-of-fact account of the storm he'd fled reminded him that he was dealing with members of the Greatest Generation, survivors of the Depression and World War II. Retired after substantial careers, they were tough and took things in stride, even in their 90's.

Curtis knew he hadn't reached the proper frame of mind for his own eminent retirement. He was still upset by loud family disagreements, angry faculty debates, the clashes of sound and color in television ads, violent movies, warrior video games. That's why he liked this quiet little town—when there were no storms, that is!

Hartford was a village in northeastern North Carolina, where a handful of family names—like Newton or Winston—could be found, Curt felt, on nearly all the houses. There had been about 1,500 residents in 1900, and the 2000 census showed the population was still 1,500. Not much had changed in a century; and everyone, like Martha Anne, knew the business of everyone else, like Edward.

Edward always seemed composed to Curt, and this one occasion of anxiety surprised him, even though the hurricane was a bad one. Curt wanted to know this local celebrity better. Irrationally perhaps, he felt Edward held a key that might help him find a golden age serenity for himself.

46

II.

He had met Edward—well, Edward had introduced himself to him—two summers ago. Curtis was raking grass seed into the fill dirt the contractor had left behind the new bulkhead in the Lindblooms' back yard. Edward was canoeing past, fishing pole in one hand, paddle in the other. Curt appreciated his smooth approach, paddle dipping without a sound.

"You like your canoe?" Edward called out, heading his boat into the wind and keeping it still. He pointed up the bank, where the Lindbloom boat, turned upside down, rested on blocks. Curt had not gotten the knack of navigating on this water, always letting the bow catch the wind and turn him off course. "It's a Grumman, isn't it?"

"Yes, I believe it is. It was my father-in-law's, and we enjoy it."

"That's a good make. I bought this one not long after I got back from the war." Edward's canoe was silver, had some dents and worn spots but was obviously seaworthy. Curtis calculated from 1945—that would make it around sixty years old.

He had seen this man before, a bowed figure in a worn straw hat, paddling along the shore. He'd marveled at Edward's ability to glide into the wind one-handed while casting, then turn around and go back the way he'd come, his course true and steady in current and breeze.

"I don't know how old that one is," admitted

Curt. "My son had it out the other day. So much quieter than the powerboats." There were few pleasure craft along this river, but clammers and bass fishermen were out early and sometimes in numbers.

Edward nodded. "You pay attention to where you are in a canoe."

"Well, today's a work day for me." Curt smiled and hefted his rake. "Got to get some grass going here before the next storm washes the dirt away." Right by the water, his yard looked oddly like desert, not a green thing growing in sandy brown soil.

"You're doing the right thing." Edward looked across at Curt's neighbor's yard, an expanse of bare dirt also. They'd done the two bulkheads at the same time, getting a good price from Joe Roddick, the local man everyone recommended. "I'm not sure Tom there should wait to seed, even though there'll be better rain in a few months."

Though he didn't look forward to mowing it, Curtis wanted grass. His outdated Briggs and Stratton machine roared through a failing muffler, but he refused to replace it until it died a natural death.

He wiped the sweat from his forehead. "They tell me I should put down sod—the geese will eat seed. But that's pretty expensive." The Canadian birds, now year-round residents, would fly over, as many as seventy-five or a hundred, an incessant honking announcing their approach from half a

48

mile away across the water.

"It's not just the seed." Edward had pulled close to the bulkhead, keeping his canoe stationary with a single paddle. "They pull it up by the roots. And they love those new shoots."

Now that he saw him up close, Curt realized Edward was older than his active life suggested. The deeply tanned skin folded up in his neck, the muscles down his arm looked stringy, and his fingers were bent, probably with some arthritis. But he had no trouble navigating, and his voice was strong, not feeble or quivery like many of the elderly people Curt knew.

He explained, "Well, seed is my only option right now."

Curtis and his wife had gone through their budget for basic repairs on the 99-year-old house in the first two years. Now each new phase would have to wait until they could save up more money. But they enjoyed preserving a local landmark and had done enough they could spend long weekends and much of the summer here.

"What you might want to do is put in some St. Augustine plugs. It's what most folks have along here." He waved down the row of old houses. Front Street ended at the old ferry landing to the north and at the Episcopal church cemetery in the south, about three blocks of homes mostly owned by families that had been here for generations.

Curt had never heard of this kind of grass, but

he associated it with the ancient Christian author of *Confessions* and *The City of God*. He guessed, though, that it came from the city in Florida.

"I'd like that, but, right now, we're kind of strapped for funds after we put in the new gas furnace and had the roof painted." He pointed up the bank. He heard the garbage truck on the other side of the house, mechanically lifting each house's bin set on the sidewalk, upending it into the crushing mechanism, thumping it back down by the curb.

Ed surveyed the Newton property. The previous owner, in her 80s, had let things go. A lot of the problems were cosmetic—faded, peeling paint; some cracked plaster; worn out fixtures in kitchen and bathroom—so they'd decided to do as much as they could themselves.

"Come down to my house," Ed said. "You can cut some plugs along the driveway and sidewalk. The grass grows up over the concrete, and edging it makes it look better."

"Why, that's very nice. I guess I'd be willing to give it a try."

"Good. When can you come?"

Curt was a little surprised at how fast this was going. He didn't want to be taking advantage of a neighbor's good will. He and Beth were among the few in this little community who were not permanent residents. "When would it suit you?"

"Tomorrow?"

50

"Okay, sure. That would be great."

"What time?"

Still wanting not to inconvenience his neighbor, Curt suspected that Edward, at his age, was probably slow rising. "Oh, I don't know ...a little after 9:00?"

"I have to be at the church to answer the phone on Friday's at that time. Earlier?"

"All right, would 7:30 work?"

"I'll be ready for you." Edward nodded, glanced out into the river, and swung the boat away from bank. In a bit of a stupor, Curt watched him, the efficient, clean paddle strokes propelling his craft cleanly through the water. It might be that Edward's gift with plants would put order in Curt's desert yard.

III.

"Tell you one thing," Curtis explained to Beth that evening, "I'm not going to be late at his house — military promptness, you know." He often joked with her about being on time, as if his two years in the Army had trained him to meet deadlines. He had been shaped more by the academic clock, meeting and dismissing classes at the bell; but he knew that Edward, like so many other men in this community, had served in the military.

"You'd better take what you need," she replied. "Everyone here will loan you their tools — or give you a spare outright!"

"I've got that big bucket we have, the short shovel, and work gloves. But now that you mention it, in order not to inconvenience Edward, I'm going to show up fifteen minutes early."

He heard helicopters cruising down the coast from the Coast Guard Station in nearby Elizabeth City. More than one, and big ones.

"Must they fly right over the house?" complained Beth, grimacing as if she were actually in pain. When the choppers flew low, they could feel the thumping of the blades like someone pounding on top of the house. Once she told Curtis she felt she'd been caught in an indoor rock concert for teenagers.

"We'll get used to it," he reminded her. "It's like living close to the train — remember Clarksville?"

They'd spent a year in Kentucky early in their marriage. He was an Army clerk at Fort Campbell, and she taught elementary school. It was a good thing she did, because, his income as a private was not enough for them to live off base. But the apartment they could afford was only a block away from constant railroad train traffic.

They had both adjusted to the regular roar of freight trains rumbling past, pausing their conversation unconsciously at the minutes of loudest noise. They were surprised every time visiting family members remarked on the disturbance.

Curtis suspected he would never be able to block out completely the passing of helicopters, reminding him, as they did, of the many flights he'd taken in Vietnam as an Army correspondent. All his rides taken to pursue stories were uneventful except one.

On that occasion he was working on a story about Rome Plows and the clearing of vegetation to protect rural roads from ambush. The Chinook he'd hitched a ride on out to an operation near Pleiku had been flying low and fast so that, Curt assumed, no one on the ground would have time to get the bird in a weapon's sight.

He was strapped in the canvas web harness next to a dozen combat engineers returning to the field. There was an explosion, the helicopter tilted sharply to one side, the giant rear cargo door dropped down, and wind and smoke rushed in. He was hanging from the wall, now more a ceiling, looking at jungle vegetation rushing by less than fifty yards beneath him.

The ship lurched, tilting back the other way, and threw Curt and the others up on their backs. He heard automatic weapon fire, perhaps friendly, perhaps not. He could see a crew member clinging with one hand to a support bar above him and yelling something, it seemed, to Curt. He couldn't hear a word in the din.

Then the helicopter leveled out. The crew member reached a lever, the cargo door cranked shut, and the noise abated to the usual howl of engines and blades. They flew smoothly to their destination. No explanation was given, none requested. It had happened so fast Curt had no time to think or act.

He never told anyone about the incident, but now, living part-time in the regular flight path of Coast Guard air traffic, he recalled his two minutes of chaos more often that he would have liked.

IV.

Curtis discovered that 7:15 a.m. wasn't early enough. He found Edward already working down his driveway with a cross between a mattock and a giant hoe, slicing a neat row of turf six inches wide against the concrete—ka-chunk, ka-chunk, ka-chunk.

"Good morning," Curt said, hurrying his last few steps. "Here, I can do that."

"Morning. I've about got it here. You pull up those pieces." Edward looked at his bucket. "That might not be big enough. Get my wheelbarrow from the side of the house there, and we'll load it up."

Curt realized he should have bought his own (brand new) wheelbarrow, but it was too late for that. When he rolled Edward's (looking as old as its owner) around the house, he found he could pull up strips of earth and grass with his hands, taking no effort at all. Edward's clean cut parallel to the cement was as effective as a perforated edge on a machine-produced mailing.

54

"This is going to be a big help. So, I just put these down ..." He hesitated. The drawbridge warning bell, fifty yards away, was clanging. The full mechanism, built in the 1920s, would creak and groan in a moment, the central stretch of bridge rotating on its circular base to open a channel on each side.

Raising his voice over the noise, Edward explained, "Plant them in plugs, maybe six inches square, perhaps a foot apart. When they're established, they'll connect. You can't buy St. Augustine seeds because they produce so few, spreading instead by their roots. It's more like one eternal plant spreading and sometimes retreating. But it will hold at your place."

"Ah. Sounds like all I'll need is rain — and a dog to keep away the geese!"

Curt looked at his neighbor, who had not broken a sweat but must have been working steadily for half an hour in the early morning heat.

Edward surveyed the sky. "You might get the rain late this afternoon." Curt could not see a cloud. "I'll come by your house later and see how you've done."

"No, please. I'll bring the wheelbarrow back and tell you how it went." He would ask Beth to put some biscuits or cookies in a tin as a thank you. If he wasn't careful, he felt, Edward would follow him home and plant the plugs himself.

"When do you go back to Virginia?" his new

friend asked.

"Sunday after church. We both teach on Mondays."

A fishing boat having passed through the draw, the bridge mechanism jolted back into action. The base rested on something like giant ball bearings, worn down over the years to the point that the entire bridge needed replacement. There was no way to get lubrication down in there, so the grinding of parts resembled the rumbling of an earthquake, often loud enough that he and Beth heard it two blocks away.

"If we don't get that rain, I'll water a bit while you're gone. You have a hose?"

"Yes. But that's too much trouble. Really, we can rely on Mother Nature."

Edward smiled, and Curt knew this man was going to come by no matter what he said. What was it about the old folks in Hartford? Ancient but active, hospitable and helpful. Whatever it was, he was going to "take the water," as they said in Jane Austen's novels.

What the village got that day was not just rain, but a thunderstorm, three inches of water in less than two hours. A Midwesterner who had been in tornados, Curt told Beth they might want to stay downstairs, close to the central hall, just in case.

"If this doesn't wash, my St. Augustine will be appropriately soaked," he remarked. Water dispersed quickly in the sandy soil.

"It seems to be coming straight down. Hear it drumming on the roof?"

The sound was loudest in the hallway, above the staircase rising to the second floor.

"Yeah, but, look out there—the devil is beating his wife."

Clouds hung low for several miles down the river, but then there was an open space through which the sun shone on the water.

"And isn't that a rainbow?"

V.

Hurricane Irene came two years later, and Curtis was pleased that he had almost no erosion behind the bulkhead. As predicted, the St. Augustine grass had spread from Edward's plugs (and more dug from other gracious neighbors). It gave Curt particular satisfaction to notice that his yard looked as good as the one next door, which had been sodded at considerable expense. "Sweat equity," he complimented himself. "It's better than cash outlay."

Edward had become a regular guest at the informal dinners Beth hosted for guests and neighbors. Having spaded up a small plot in the side yard, Curt plied Edward for gardening advice. He was always behind his friend in starting seeds indoors, staking plants, putting in cover crops for the winter, but he was learning how working the soil soothed the soul.

It amused Curt to find that Edward's latest new project was planting bald cypress seedlings along the back row of his property. They grow well in the swampy areas of the state, their knees poking up in the shallow creeks and coves all around Hartford.

Curt reported his friend's efforts to Beth, who loved the four giant cypress that stood in a row between the Newton house and the water.

"What do they take to mature, a hundred years?" she asked.

"Probably, but Ed says in twenty years one can be up over 40 feet high."

"So, he'll be able to sit in their shade when he's — what? — 115."

Curt smiled. "I'm not betting against it happening!"

At one of their dinners, the conversation turned to experiences in war. Curt had heard that Edward has been in World War II, but he'd been reluctant to ask for details. One of their guests, Ben Svensson, had been a Navy pilot in the Vietnam era. Edward asked what planes he flew and then offered, "I was in a B-24. Rear gunner."

Curt said, "I can't imagine what that must have been like."

"It was pretty bad. Some boys, after one mission, wouldn't go up again. 'Court martial, me,' they said. 'Or just shoot me,' but I'm not going up there a second time." He shook his head, as if he understood but had known how to deal with it himself.

Curt remembered a scene from *Catch-22*, the WW II movie. Yossarian, on a bombing mission over Europe, takes off his earphones when he hears a call from the pilot to "help him!" He doesn't know who "him" is or what has happened, but leaves his post to look. He finds a fellow crew member lying on his back, injured in some way.

The wind whips at Yossarian's clothes and whistles around the wounded Snowden. When Yosarrian tries to make him warmer by covering him with a parachute, he finds that the man's torso has been ripped open by flak and his innards are tumbling out. Yossarrian's mouth is wide in a silent scream, but only the engines roar.

Ben asked Edward, "How many missions did you fly?"

"We were shot down after thirteen. But it was late in the war, and we all got out through Russia."

Ben's eyes widened. "Got out? Well, I hope that meant you were done flying missions."

"We went back up, but more on supply flights, not to bomb. Of course, the people on the ground couldn't always tell the difference."

No one quite knew how to respond. Edward, rubbing his chin, continued. "I've never seen such hungry people, the Russians. Makes you grateful." He smiled, and Beth, sensing the moment, rose, too.

"I think we can go to the table now."

When she asked Edward if he would say grace, their guest took the hands of those next to him and they all joined in a circle of bowed heads. He thanked God for the many blessings of friends and food and comfort. Then he reminded them all to remember those who are suffering and in need of care.

VI.

Before going upstairs to bed that night, Curtis stood alone on the deck for a few moments and looked across his yard of St. Augustine grass. A full moon had risen over the water and illuminated the landscape. There was no wind, and the water, smooth as a mirror, showed a path of light reaching up to the bulkhead.

The grass was lush, and, though he couldn't see color, he knew it was a rich, deep green. Oddly, he concluded that the full lawn tonight had calmed the river, the trees, himself. He remembered taking the first plug from Edward's wheelbarrow and planting it in the fill dirt. He had wondered if it would take.

"From his hands to my hands," Curtis said to himself. "From his earth to mine. This is holy grass."

# "The Voice of God"

He thought of her as "The Voice of God" because when he first heard her sing — sing, that is, as she had been trained — she was in the pulpit above and behind him, invisible but compelling.

He was one of fifty-some local church choir members who twice a year created a community chorus. Their director, a music professor at the local college, called in soloists, who rehearsed separately; so Mark didn't know whose voice struck him so profoundly in that final rehearsal before the performance. He was surprised to realize that he had actually met the attractive soprano.

The group was moving this year beyond the standard repertoire — Handel's *Messiah*, Brahms' *Requiem* — to perform Ralph Vaughan William's *Dona Nobis Pacem* (Grant us Peace), composed in the 1930s as the world headed for a second global war. Mark was pleased at the choice since the conflict in Iraq had taken not one but a number of ugly turns. While soldiers and civilians were dying thousands of miles away, most Americans were going about business as usual. He longed for a wake-up call and somehow felt it in Deborah's voice. *Agnus Dei, qui tollis peccata mundi, miserere nobis.*

At the end of the rehearsal, when he saw the soloist, he wasn't sure this slender, young brunette could be the Gabriel the nation needed — too young, too beautiful, too bright. He also realized with some embarrassment that Deborah had come to a couple of his church choir practices.

Mark had taken no particular notice of her, struggling with his own part as always; he didn't read music well and always searched for the pitch. Never mentioning that she had a degree in voice, Deborah molded her singing to match the other sopranos. She asked for help with difficult or unusual passages and laughed at her own goofs. So when he finally turned at the rehearsal for *Dona Nobis Pacem* and saw whose voice had filled every crevice in the church, he was stunned. The unassuming young woman from his church had been transformed into a commanding presence.

Deborah's heart was in the music, Mark's in Walt Whitman poetry, the cantata's text, which laments the tragedy of war. Whitman's compassion for soldiers came from his service as a hospital volunteer in the American Civil War; Ralph Vaughan Williams was a veteran of World War I.

Congratulating Deborah at the reception after the final performance, Mark learned that she had put her musical career on hold while raising three small children. More startling to him, she was now thinking of going into nursing.

"With all your education and your talent?" He was also assuming she would be motivated by a conventional American desire for expensive homes, cars, possessions.

She smiled, dipping a carrot in the hummus. "I helped look after my grandfather in a nursing home. I thought we could do better in this country for those who are ill. I have to go back to school first to get the right science courses, but I can do that at night."

*Right*, thought Mark, knowing well the nursing curriculum at his own institution—*in five to seven years*! Aloud he said, "You can't take care of everyone yourself."

"Oh," she laughed, taking a sip of sweet tea. "I'll care for them one at a time."

Mark was a Vietnam veteran, one of the last of the draftee generation, and understood how much caring would be needed for the soldiers taking multiple tours in the Middle East and for their families back home. Deborah's brother, it turned out, had done twenty years in the Navy.

Unlike the situations of the American Civil War and Europe's two world wars, only a small portion of American society was paying the costs of these conflicts. Everyone else seemed to following President Bush's advice to "go to the mall." And Mark felt this war was as much about stocking the mall as making the world safe for democracy.

He cautioned, "A nursing degree can be expensive, even at a public university."

"I've already started teaching a music appreciation course online. And my children are good sleepers; I get most of that work done in the evenings."

How did she have such energy? Her husband was a new biology professor at his own school. That was a hard department to get tenure in; and junior faculty put in long hours on laboratory or field research. Mark worried that Deborah had little help at home.

The couple was about the age of his own children. And when Mark sang the words to "Dirge for Two Veterans," he thought about the sufferings of generations. "*I hear a sad procession, / And I hear the sound of coming full-keyed bugles,*" laments the piece. "*Two veterans, son and father, dropped together/ And the double grave awaits them.*" While a father in the national guard—or a mother—might have a child on active duty today, Mark felt the nation at large would not grieve their falling as they should.

Moved by Deborah's desire to serve others, he decided to write a brief informational piece about Whitman and Williams, about citizen soldiers and shared sacrifice, about social divisions and individual commitment. He would offer it to the director for inclusion in the concert program. Would this add to Deborah's voice and to the singers' choruses? Would they change the world? Unlikely.

Still, he thought later, perhaps it had helped, after all. His words were printed and Deborah sang. Who knew? In other communities awareness might be spreading as it had with them. The media could decide to give more time to wounded

64

warriors, to programs supporting their families, to the case for spending more on military and civilian healthcare. Fewer people might be looking for the next war, for the next chance to demonize a person or a group, for more sophisticated weapons of mass destruction. It could happen.

Mark knew it was idealistic to see peace on earth in his or his children's lifetime. But he had heard The Voice of God. And he had to believe.

# Magician

I.

When James heard the *thumpa-thumpa-thumpa* of the approaching helicopter's blades, he had an immediate, warmly nostalgic flashback to his Missouri childhood and a game of cops-and-robbers.

"I hope it's not my life flashing before my eyes," he whispered with a low chuckle to Martin. Then he allowed the sights and sounds of forty years ago to carry him away from the present into the magical world of memory.

II.

"Bang! You're dead," Jimmy heard Marty yell. He had just poked his head above the hood of the Johnsons' 1952 Buick, looking for enemies (the cops).

Jimmy (a robber) tried, of course, the customary dodge: "You missed me! You missed me!" Then he ducked back down behind the car, preparing to rise and shoot his friend.

But Marty would not allow the familiar evasion. "No! I got you. You're dead."

"Okay, okay," Jimmy thought; he would be "dead" this time. Shrugging his shoulders, he rose before the leveled cork rifle of the enemy, who had stepped around the large oak tree in the Berrys' front yard, and prepared to be marched off to base. The base was the Picketts' side porch, where all the "dead" or captured robbers had to go. After all, Jimmy knew, play would be going on throughout the day and even into the evening. Others would soon get shot; and new rounds of the game would begin in which Jimmy would be "alive" again.

Versions of hide-and-seek were being played out all over America in these (apparently) peaceful times of the 1950s, in small towns like this and in the bigger cities of Springfield (100 miles to the west along fabled Route 66) and St. Louis (100 miles east on the same highway). With no school in the long summer months, this group of marauders was completely free, too young even for chores like mowing lawns or the job of a paper route. Neighborhood play followed ancient patterns but also adjusted to the historically recent conflict of World War II. The official game today had been "Cops and Robbers," but on other days the kids were "Cowboys and Indians," "GI's and Japs," "Germans and Americans."

This homogeneous gang of Middle Americans always divided themselves into two opposing groups—good and bad, them and us, one side and the other—though no one looking on could have told the difference from their appearance. Even boy and girl dressed the same and copied each other's speech, action, behavior.

When he joined Susan and Kathy on the porch, Jimmy was already sensing the distant, punctuated drone of the approaching helicopter: *thumpa-thumpa-thumpa*. He did not yet realize he was hearing it; nor would he at first distinguish the sound from the different noises made by more familiar, single-engine aircraft up above the clouds. But before the "cops" could finish rounding up "robbers," all the kids had picked up on the sound. And they began to hope the day was going to bring something new, something exciting, something memorable, into their world.

Now Jimmy heard distinctly the sound of rotor blades, the approach of a helicopter: *thumpa-thumpa-thumpa*.

"Listen," he said to the girls. "It's coming to the eye hospital."

Susan's and Kathy's faces brightened. They, too, knew this would be an event to mark the summer day as special. They leaped off the porch, meeting Bill, Sam, Marty, and Judy, who had just heard the helicopter. They raced down Limestone Street to the place where they could cut over the railroad tracks to the town's major east-west road, Kingshighway (Business Route 66). On the other side of America's "Mother Road" was the glaucoma hospital.

Even as he ran, though, Jimmy resumed a private fantasy he had been entertaining in recent weeks. This childhood wondering probably did not take distinct shape forty years later in the mind of the adult James. But it was for the adult, hearing another helicopter, one thread in a rich fabric of nostalgic associations.

III.

The young Jimmy Doubleday — earlier a robber alive in hiding, then a dead man on the porch, now a real boy racing toward the sound of a helicopter — was thinking about Mandrake the Magician, that comic strip character whose story both intrigued and baffled him. Especially in the Sunday paper, where the strip was in color (rather than the weekday black-and-white), the substance and power of Mandrake haunted this uncomplicated, literal-minded boy.

If you took the cartoon frames in *Mandrake* at face value, Jimmy understood, you saw the hero divert an avalanche with a mere wave of the hand or catch a hurtling arrow and shoot it back to the man holding a bow. Yet the strip's premise was that this magician was merely a supreme hypnotist and his amazing feats of skill simple acts of illusion. The avalanche still came; Mandrake had just stepped out of its way. The arrow did not reverse its flight and home in on the archer; it had simply missed a moving Mandrake.

Jimmy was initially happy when he figured out the comic strip's principles: the newspaper drawings represented what Mandrake's victims, under hypnosis, *thought* was happening. Readers had to fill in for themselves much of what was really going on.

Because Mandrake's powers did not exist in fact, only in illusion, they appeared, by a process of inverted child logic, to be potentially available to Jimmy himself.

If he could just wave his hand in the right way, abbreviating the traditional hypnotist's swinging a pocket watch in front of the subject's eyes, Jimmy could make Marty's imaginary bullet seem, even to a boy holding a cork rifle, to sail past its target. Or, still better, Marty would be made to forget that he had ever seen Jimmy pop up behind the Buick. He would instead hear Jimmy call out to him, "Bang! You're dead," and sadly acknowledge that his friend had won this round of the game.

On the other hand, that Mandrake could not control or manipulate reality was unsettling. The strength to lift a jeep or the speed to outrun a train was something any eight-year-old boy dreamed of somehow having in his own future manhood. If such a superior being only seemed invulnerable, however, what chances did an 85-pound kid have of escaping attack and defeat in a world populated by so many larger and stronger opponents?

As a man and a father, James Doubleday came to understand a child's sense of smallness in a world of grownups by observing and listening to his own sons. Like most men, of course, he did not always remember that adults are small in the face of world events, sickness, and accident.

III.

The little group of seven adventurers in 1954 — none of them Mandrake — was unable to reach the empty field next door to the glaucoma hospital in

70

time to see the helicopter land in the parking lot. But they were there before the motor cut off and the blades swung finally to a stop. They saw a black man (they would call him a "Negro") in a uniform helping a white man in a long coat (perhaps a hospital gown) with a bandage wrapped around his eyes. Holding his arm, the attendant escorted the patient into the two-story brick building, one of the largest in this town of 11,000.

Only one of the children—Susan, who had lived in Louisville before moving to Missouri— had ever known a black person. This small town had only a handful of African-American residents until after 1960, when several families, inspired by the blossoming Civil Rights movement, fled decayed neighborhoods of St. Louis. They did not find universal acceptance in communities like Fairfield.

"Who's the guy in bandages?" whispered Judy.

Marty asked, "Why is he coming here? Is this an emergency?"

"Who was that ...other guy?" wondered Susan, vaguely uncomfortable about using the "N" word, which she would have in other circumstances.

Sammy, the group's know-it-all, concluded, "The man is blind. He's going to get some kind of special treatment and be able to see again."

Jimmy, wanting to be in the discussion, said, "No, I bet this guy's going to have to live the rest of his life in a hospital or something. And there's more wrong with him. He won't live very long.

"Oh!" lamented Judy.

The kids never learned about this man's fate. During the time the two men were approaching the hospital building, the children had been unconsciously inching forward across the grounds. They were perhaps thirty feet from the doorway and standing beneath some small ornamental trees when the black man spotted them. He spoke in a stern but not angry voice. "You chil'ren better get on 'way from here."

They were used to being shooed out of people's yards, told to leave stores where they had no money to spend, herded by parents and teachers from one place to another. In fact, being sent away often meant that they had achieved some kind of success: broken a rule aimed at keeping them from enjoying an unknown pleasure or passed through a boundary intended to limit their understanding. So, even as they retreated, they felt that getting close to the helicopter had been a significant accomplishment. And the powerful images of that July afternoon stayed with Jimmy for four decades and came back now strongly in his forty-ninth year …

IV.

James was going to ask Martin if he remembered that moment from their past, but then he realized the helicopter that had reminded him of the childhood event was now as close as the one he had seen at the glaucoma hospital. And before he could get out the question to Martin, a second memory, more powerful than the first, swept over him. This Vietnam experience had come back infrequently but powerfully in his life.

V.

"You're dead!" said Jim to Martin near dawn in January 1968. He had just made what he thought was a final move.

"I don't think so," responded Martin.

The two had enlisted in the Army under a buddy program, knowing that they were due to be drafted soon anyway and wanting at least to choose their training. As promised by a local recruiter, they did travel together through boot camp (at nearby Fort Leonard Wood), advanced training in electronics (Fort Hood, Texas), and duty along the coast of the South China Sea. As clerks in the signal corps, they spent twelve relatively safe months moving some information and more paperwork through division headquarters.

Their few moments as combat soldiers came on guard duty, when sappers occasionally tested the perimeter of their large support base and when early morning mortar fire found its way into the compound. Even then, however, veterans from the bush, who manned the forward towers, took control of all serious situations. And the rear echelon troops in Jim's company remained at less vulnerable positions.

That any genuine threat might materialize on their watch seemed a remote possibility, especially after their first six months in country. Having finished two years of college and being older than many of their fellow enlisted men, they had found themselves less and less respectful of S.O.P. (standard operating procedure). Like most support personnel there, they counted on the enormous distance in this war between the rear—where regulations were slack—and the boonies—where military discipline mattered.

On their most memorable moment in Vietnam, the night of their helicopter experience, Martin uncovered a bomb at the place of Jim's attack.

Perhaps the most outrageous violation of security performed by clerks in their company involved carrying games out to the bunker to pass the time during the frequently uneventful six hours of guard duty (6:00 p.m.—or "1800 hours"—to midnight; or "2400 hours" to 6:00 a.m.). Many of the enlisted men hid small radios or paperback books in the large pockets of their fatigues; and everyone took snacks. But Jim and Martin began near the end of their tour to take a homemade war game out on guard duty.

Drawing on memories of childhood board games, they had created their own entertainment: a folding cardboard map of Vietnam marked off in a grid, plus thirty pieces representing troops, land mines, artillery, and headquarters. The two positioned their units on the map to protect their home bases. Each player could see the emblem

74

(stick-figure soldier, bomb with smoking fuse, cannon, flag) facing him on his own pieces; but they both had to guess at the hidden character of the enemy's.

"Wait a minute," questioned Jim when Martin explained he was not dead. "I thought you'd used up all your mines." Martin, a mischievous look on his face, was chewing a peanut butter bar.

"You miscounted." Martin turned his piece around to show the bomb. "That was my last one. Now it's my turn."

In "Pacification" (their ironic name for this board game) Jim and Martin traded turns firing at each other by identifying locations on the grid as targets, with the goal of knocking out enemy defenses, destroying opposing soldiers, and eventually blowing up the other player's headquarters. Strategy, if there were any, involved the placement of the headquarters flag among offensive and defensive units and keeping track of the other player's pieces.

Sometimes when he played "Pacification," Jim recalled his childhood comic hero, Mandrake. He thought of catching Martin with the celebrated hypnotic gesture, putting him to sleep. Then he could make his opponent turn all his pieces around, revealing their identities to Jim. When he awoke from Jim's spell, Martin would never understand why defeat came so swiftly, so inevitably.

Martin, pulling out a second peanut butter bar,

75

now fired at Jim. "This ought to put you in a world of hurt." But even as he made this announcement he looked up and out of the bunker at the sound of an approaching aircraft: *thumpa-thumpa-thumpa*.

Although Jim believed having the abilities of Mandrake would win games of "Pacification" and more, he also carried from his childhood the old uncertainty about form and illusion associated with this fictional character. His confusion was related to the way the colors missed the black outlines in the Sunday comic strips.

In those days, colors were added in the newspaper printing operation as paper passed under successive plates: first black (as with regular type) onto the white newsprint, then primary colors in an order that allowed overlay (say of yellow on blue) to multiply the number of shades (yielding, for instance, green). But often the images were not precisely aligned, and a blue shadow might hover behind Mandrake, or a ribbon of red would outline a fallen man. All the parts of the strip were there; but an out-of-phase arrangement underscored Jim's inability to grasp the artist's vision.

And now his own vision was being tested by a sound: *thumpa-thumpa-thumpa*.

Out of a habit born in the last month and triggered by the noise of an approaching flyer, Jim picked up a camera and sighted through the slit in their bunker across the perimeter with its rolls of concertina war.

"Time out," he announced to Martin, suspending the game.

"Time out? When you're about to loose!"

Like a lot of other clerical personnel in Vietnam, Jim had been bitten by the technology bug — Japanese electronic equipment available through base PX's at less than half the usual stateside prices. The 35-millimeter Pentax with telephoto and wide-angle lenses was the latest in a series of purchases — stereos, tape players, receivers — meant to amuse Jim during off-duty hours.

He had not been a photographer before Vietnam, of course. And he would loose interest by the time he landed in Oakland several months later. But for some weeks, one more version of the ugly American looked at and recorded on film dozens of sights in this new world; he was never genuinely interested in his subject, simply keeping a record of what came into his field of vision.

"Where's he going?" wondered Martin. He too had become interested in the helicopter.

"Where is that guy?" asked Jim, sweeping left and right with his camera.

The little observation chopper he and Martin soon spotted, with pilot and copilot visible in its bubble body — the copilot leaning awkwardly to one side — was flying oddly low to the ground, no more than 25 feet high, and coming fast at them on about a 45-degree angle from right to left.

Confused about that distance and still unpracticed with his camera, Jim spun the barrel trying to get the bird in focus.

After their increased development and deployment for the Korean conflict, American helicopters were always in the air in this war: big, banana-shaped chinooks transporting troops and material; the familiar Hueys on routine mail runs; menacing cobras searching and destroying the enemy with rapid-fire mini-guns. So a picture of the one Jim and Martin were hearing would only add to a collection of usually out-of-focus prints. Still, Pentax to eye, Jim scanned the sky before him, which was just brightening in the first stages of dawn.

"He's mighty low," observed Martin.

"I can't get him," Jim complained, trying to fix the chopper in his viewfinder.

When an object was not in focus, Jim's Pentax viewfinder presented two images. The operator had to lengthen or shorten the camera barrel—unscrewing or screwing it in by turning a ring in its middle—until the two images were exactly superimposed, producing a clear picture. Although Jim got the little bug in sight, he couldn't turn the ring fast enough to bring the two images together as the helicopter continued to move. The chopper, in fact, at that very moment shot directly overhead, almost pulling Jim onto his back as he tracked its rapid flight. And then all hell broke loose.

It was the Tet offensive of 1968, the

coordinated, country-wide attack on U.S. bases and important South Vietnamese cities that, more than any single military event, turned American public opinion against the war. This particular battle began with concentrated rocket fire, punctuated by incoming rounds from closer mortar positions. And Jim and Martin crouched down in the bunker in fundamental panic as rockets went past and shells whistled into the compound.

U.S. artillery and planes countered swiftly in Martin and Jim's area. The two young men had their moments of terror, during which they tried unsuccessfully to get the bunker's M-60 machine gun loaded and operational. But neither they nor their limited firepower proved necessary after the effective response of combat trained forces.

The sound and blurred picture of the one scout helicopter racing ahead of enemy fire marked dramatically Jim's experience of war. And today, a quarter of a century later, the *thumpa-thumpa-thumpa* of the emergency medical helicopter coming to land beside the highway, Interstate 44 near Waynesville, brought back that memory.

The perhaps ten minutes of fear Jim endured on the day of Tet marked one of the few times he had come close to realizing he could be a casualty in war time. Amazingly, he knew individuals from his own company who were killed, read accounts of soldiers lost in combat, and saw wounded men being transported to overseas hospitals or home without ever fully understanding that he could easily have been in their place. It might have been considered a gift, an ability to avoid high anxiety. But it was also an elemental ignorance that, in circumstances other than his comfortable assignment, might have gotten him killed.

VI.

"You're dead," Martin said to James, nervously hoping, that because they were both going to be all right, he could make a joke. But James did not answer right away. He was slumped to one side, stunned.

"Now's the time for magic," he thought to himself, once again reviewing the power of Mandrake. He meant to wave a hand, sweep away the automobile crash.

Actually, it was not a completely illogical thought in this crisis. Martin had never given up his childhood love of the comics and often thought of himself as a magician, able to reshape reality. He had become a successful political cartoonist. He drew the world to suit his convictions three times a week for some thousands of newspapers readers. The boxed frame on the editorial page was an agent of illusion with which he, like Mandrake, could make people react to something that was not there, make them fail to see what was before them in reality.

"Here's the rescue guys," Martin shouted over the roar of the aircraft. "You'll be out of here in no time. Taken care of. All right."

While Martin was uninjured, the air bag on

James's side of the car had failed to function. He'd been thrown forward toward the windshield and then bounced off the doorframe as the car rolled into the ditch. It was Friday afternoon, and they'd been headed for Martin's cabin on the Lake of the Ozarks, a weekend of fishing and reminiscing.

"What?" asked Jim, unable to hear over the helicopter's roar: *thumpa-thumpa-thumpa*. His vision was blurred now too. He couldn't move.

Jim's career as a cartoonist had risen as the Cold War deepened. At its heyday, about five years ago, his work had been syndicated in many Midwestern states. Later, the number of subscribers had begun a steady decline. The fall of the Berlin Wall and the collapse of the Soviet Union seemed to have blocked Jim's creativity. His exaggerated figures representing Communism versus Capitalism had gone out of date. And he couldn't find a new style. Still, he hadn't lost faith in his powers.

He never resolved all his doubts about Mandrake the Magician, however. Not many years ago another item of contradiction in the strip had begun to puzzle him. While the comic hero was always resolving conflicts — fashioning a wire cage into which escaping bank burglars unwittingly walked, disarming would-be muggers with amazing swiftness — Mandrake also never ran out of problems.

What good, questioned Jim, were all the magician's skills if every week a new danger rose up to challenge him and civilization? Why couldn't his great gift eventually win him and the world some peace? This hero's life was always in crisis and never turned to simple pleasure or relaxation—a weekend at the lake.

Now, as two of the white-clad emergency personnel prepared to lift him from the seat and place him on a stretcher, Jim smiled and said, "This won't be necessary."

The rescue crew stopped what they were doing, puzzled looks on their faces.

"I'm fine," Jim said and swung his legs out of the car. The men stumbled back out of his way.

"Don't hurry it," said Martin, though he was clearly relieved. He had feared the worst.

"I tell you I'm fine. Just got the wind knocked out of me. Momentary loss of focus." The feeling had returned in his arms and legs. There was no pain; everything worked; he *was* a magician!

"Make sure you're okay, though." Martin put a hand on Jim's shoulder, cautioning. The medical men wanted to take his blood pressure, look into his eyes for signs of concussion, feel his bones for fractures, bleeding. He held up a hand: not necessary.

The helicopter's motors must have been cut off, as everything was becoming still. He thought again of the playmates of his childhood, chasing each other in summer games of hide-and-seek. He could almost hear their cries of joy as they played on past sunset and into the cool dark of evening.

Jim stood, shook his rescuers by the hand. They retreated toward the helicopter and the rescue vehicles, surprised but happy to find an accident without casualties. In their uniforms they reminded him of soldiers, tired soldiers he'd seen in Vietnam. But they were far from that conflict now. The frantic radio calls for dust-offs could be forgotten: the stand down was permanent. A wave of happiness for them almost overcame him.

He turned to Martin. It was not too late to make it to the cabin tonight, if they could get the car fixed or find a replacement. He gazed over the Ozark hills to the west, still outlined by the last glimmers of daylight. He was a lucky man. He knew that life had been kind to him. He made one last sweeping gesture with his hand, and a wonderful peace descended on everything.

# Stratego

After that time near Katum, Copy started to make his own Stratego game. He traded cassettes for poster stock from Bob, one of the photographers, and drew the board. Then, keeping himself out of sight in the sound booth, he made the pieces, designing symbols for the different officers, the bombs, the flags. It took a while for the others to make the connection: a war game and an actual firefight.

All the audio specialists used the sound booth to hide things—letters they were writing, books of a decidedly unmilitary nature, personal music tapes they copied to send home (taking advantage of free air shipment for U.S. military overseas). They would sit behind the glass in front of the microphone as if about to begin a recording session when, in fact, they were entertaining themselves with their own interests. It was all, as they said, part of their "military strategy."

Among other guidelines carried down from one generation of clerks to the next in the era of the draft:

Hand-carry all personal papers.

In transit, always grip a manilla folder, even if empty.

Frequently request clarification.

When in doubt, come to attention and let your eyes go out of focus.

The enlisted men lucky enough to end up handling paperwork could not refuse orders, but they could often obfuscate, redirect, or delay their implementation. And they knew how.

When he'd caught a ride from Long Binh to Cu Chi, Copy thought he was going out on a routine story about Donut Dollies who entertained troops. He planned to watch one of the audience participation programs and then interview a new member of the team. A friend back home had written him, saying if he ever, by any chance, ran into Christine Rule, he should say hello. She was a sweetie.

Copy, a good reporter, drew on the established network — personnel specialists, information specialists, pay records specialists — and a generic list of interview questions. He located her within a week of her arrival.

"Tough assignment," he said winking to Standby/Stanley. (All their names had been transformed to radio terminology. Copy was really Cody.)

"You should be able to get the basic job done in what ...two days tops?"

"Well, to do it right — in depth, you know — could take a bit longer. I'll need quite a bit of studio time, too, for editing, adding sound effects, lead, close."

Wilco (William) chimed in. "Ah, strategy, my man, strategy!"

There was an unspoken agreement among the correspondents to keep expectations about their production low. They worked with deliberation and explained to Top that composing a good feature required a lot of research, review, revision. They didn't know for a long time that Top saw through their game.

"Guess where I'm off to today?" asked Roger-So-Far.

Standby suggested, "Your rocker?"

"Nope, but I bet they have them there. 24th Evac." This was a Long Binh base hospital.

"Ah, so you *are* looney tunes," concluded Wilco, twirling an index finger at his temple.

"You couldn't guess: hometowners."

Home town news releases (hometowners) were standard announcements of promotion, transfer, training sent to news agencies back in the States. The fixed format irritated the HQ enlisted men, most of whom had more flexibility in their civilian writing jobs — or thought they should have; but the strict formula made the work easy.

Copy congratulated Roger-so-Far. "Good job! You'll get to talk with the nurses while I romance the ladies of the Red Cross."

"Well, it's not my main mission, which is to interview patients; but somebody's got to take me to them. And I figure the ladies in white can check my vital signs, review my symptoms, and fix …what ails me, if you know what I mean."

Standby reminded him. "Follow protocol, Troop: fingers extended and joined, correct trigger control must be employed, utilize tried-and-tested pick-up lines."

Copy thought for a moment. "Aren't most of the bad cases shipped out to Japan A.S.A.P?"

"That's S.O.P. I'll be interviewing those with superficial injuries or routine sickness — minor flesh wound, appendicitis, jock itch — things they know how to treat."

"Well, Wilco, that leaves you to do the daily feeds. And to devise a step-by-step fantasy consummation with the Playmate of the month." Old issues of the magazine were stashed (in a file labeled "Teases") at the back of the sound booth. Copy's friend back home said Christine was as good looking as any of those girls.

After the trip, not only did Copy begin to build his own game, he researched Stratego's history, calling guys he knew at other bases and sending inquiries to family back home. It quickly became an obsession.

"Milton Bradley's Stratego derives from ancient China," he reported thoughtfully. "'Game of the Fighting Animals.' Later there was a more complicated version, 'Lu Zhan Jun Qi,' Army Chess."

Standby asked, "What's your approach, following that model or the current American product?"

"A little of both. Then, there's the French *L'attaque!* a game patented two ...no, three wars ago. Huh! I almost dropped Korea from the list of glorious conflicts in our century." They noticed that his voice had an odd coldness. Later they would remember.

The object of all versions of Stratego was to conquer the enemy, capturing the opponent's flag. The two players' pieces — bombs, military figures of different rank, the flag — are arranged on opposite sides of a 10X10 grid (the board) with their value or identity hidden from the opponent. Pieces advance in alternating moves, besting other pieces or being destroyed until the flag is seized.

The men had played in the World, and each had a favorite strategy: Standby liked his flag in the corner, protected by powerful pieces; Roger-So-Far would put his out front and count on his opponent pushing past it to the back row; Wilco claimed to be unpredictable. Copy wouldn't discuss his tactics, just kept cutting, gluing, and drawing.

"You gonna' print up a rules booklet, too?" asked Roger-So-Far one day. "That might be hard to get right from memory."

"I hadn't thought of doing it, but great idea. I'll ask my brother if he can find our old set and send me the rules. Of course, I'd still have to make my own copy."

88

"Why? I mean, the goal is to play Stratego when you finish the set, isn't it?"

"Maybe. Right now, I'm focused on construction, building a reasonable facsimile."

"Gonna' make the original box?"

"Oh, yeah. Got to have a box. That's going to take some time!"

The others could talk among themselves when he was in the sound booth, and Wilco was the first to express concern. "He's spending more and more time in there. You think he's okay?"

Standby scratched his head. "There are long periods when he doesn't even look up. Got his head down. I *guess* he's doing something ..."

The sound booth's double-pane window formed the top half of the outer wall. There was a counter waist-high inside, but it wasn't visible from across the production room where the giant reel-to-reel production machines and several desks were positioned. The announcers put the microphones and their scripts on the counter, hiding their own interests underneath (their "privates," they said).

"I think he's kind of zoned out some of the time." Roger-So-Far paused. "You know what I think? I think something happened on that Donut Dollie story. He hasn't written a word, and he's been back what ...ten days?"

"I heard him transfer the cassettes onto a 10-inch reel," explained Wilco. "There's good stuff there. This girl—Christine something—is all bright and cheery. And he's got great recordings of her yukking it up with troops out at the firebase. Of course, he could have brought us back a dozen donuts."

"Maybe he can't figure out how to shape the piece. You know, a good tease for the start, how to finish." He grinned. "Could be writer's block." This, of course, was one of their regular excuses for working slowly.

"Hasn't ever happened to him before. He usually comes back almost as if he composed the story on the way in—beginning, middle, and end all figured out, like they actually taught him how to do it at DINFOS back in Indianapolis."

Copy had signed up on the eve of being drafted so he could get a 71R20 MOS and take the skills into a civilian career after his service. The enlistment deal guaranteed training at the Defense Information School, Fort Benjamin Harrison. The other three had journalism degrees or civilian experience and reshaped their skills for the military with on-the-job training. They liked to tease him that he had a secret plan: to re-up and become a lifer.

A few days later, Standby announced a clue. "He fired his pistol, out near Katum."

The other two were stunned. Regulation required each correspondent to carry a weapon when traveling on assignment, generally a Colt 45, the M1911 pistol. No one wanted to be in a situation where it had to be used, but they dutifully qualified on the firing range every six months. The instructor invariably criticized their technique.

"How do you know?" asked Roger-So-Far.

"Top told me. It has to be reported, but he wouldn't say anything about 'where, when, and why'" — three of the standard "W" questions that guide reporters in covering a story.

"Shee-it!" Wilco concluded. "But look, we should find a way to learn what the hell happened. He's still not doing jack on his story, just polishing up his Stratego game. Yesterday, he threw away his first generation pieces and started making new ones. Said they weren't strong enough to last."

Copy had initially cut a shallow groove across the middle of a one-inch square of poster board and glued another one-inch piece standing up in the slot. From the side, it formed an upside down T, with its identity (bomb, military figure, etc.) pictured on one side, the other (seen by the opponent) a gothic letter S for Stratego. Now he was doubling the thickness of the base.

"He's also writing and rewriting the rule book every time he hears from someone. And he's integrated some special provisions from the Chinese game."

"In other words," concluded Standby, "he's going off his rocker."

Wilco concluded, "We better talk to Top again."

First Sergeant Corse was the company's senior enlisted man, called "Top" as such NCO's were by custom. Because he unobtrusively worked to keep them from being sent into dangerous situations, the men had come to respect him.

Top knew this war was approaching an end; and, like some combat commanders, he didn't want one of his men to be the last to die in Vietnam. This was also his own final overseas tour, and he looked forward to pursuing a retirement dream: setting up a fishing camp on land he and his wife had bought in Alaska.

"Yeah, I know what happened," he told Roger-So-Far, who was selected to ask about Copy. "You all want to hear, huh?"

"We're not sure he's okay. Kind of unfocused, out of it, but we don't know what to do."

"All right. Tell Standby and Wilco, roll call, the recording studio, 0800 hours on Wednesday."

"But Copy ...?"

"He won't be there."

They were reassured but puzzled. And when their colleague was sent out on a story the next day, no one seemed to know where. At the meeting on Wednesday, Top explained everything.

"Here it is, men. Specialist Brock, the Dollies, and the escort troops took a truck out of Katum to an even more remote post. Shouldn't have done so, even with a squad for security. But the girl — Miss

Rule, was it? — was so damned enthusiastic, wanted to do her part, bless her."

The men had seen Donut Dollies passing out pastry and coffee at USO centers in Long Binh and on other bases. But because of their own relatively comfortable assignments, they didn't feel the need for the same morale boosts that the grunts did and tended not to pay much attention to these Red Cross volunteers.

Top went on. "She was well prepared, even though she'd just been in-country a few weeks. She knew how to be bubbly and excited and get the men to play along. But they should have stayed away from the last post. They were ambushed on the way back."

They'd all imagined something like this happening to themselves, but could never fully conceptualize the reality. And their training hadn't instilled a true readiness.

"They let the lead vehicle go past, opened up on the truck. She took a round right in the heart — sitting up too straight, leading every one in a song. Two others were wounded before the infantry guys opened up."

"Jeez! What the hell do you do when that happens? I guess Copy used the 45."

"Well, if you're talking strategy ..." smiled Top grimly. "When the shit breaks loose, you put your head down, point whatever you've got that goes bang, and shoot at wherever bullets are coming from. At that point, there ain't no goddamned such a thing as strategy."

They were all silent. Then Wilco admitted, "I doubt if I'd have gotten off a round. And, if I did, I don't know where it would have gone."

"Then what?" asked Standby.

"Charlie retreated into the bush. It was over in less than two minutes."
Again, they didn't know what to say.

"So what's to be done with Copy?" asked Roger-So-Far gently.

Top pushed his back against the door to make sure it was closed tight. "You didn't hear this from me, okay? But here's what will happen: I sent Copy to Malaysia for a week. They've got major floods down there, and the Army is sending relief supplies and choppers to get people off of hilltops. He's going to interview the pilots and the crews, but stay on the ground in Kuala Lumpur. Even got him a room in a hotel, bed and all."

"Get his mind off Katum?"

"Roger that. And while he's gone, Wilco, you take his tapes, do the story. Leave out any names, just talk about Dollies and Special Services personnel. Standby, help him with the script. And, of course, nothing about the ambush. I want it done and shipped out to AFN before Copy returns."

"Got it."

"By the time he gets back and has the flood

story together, he'll be short." He smiled. "Especially the way you guys work."

They looked down.

"After that I'll keep him on base and hope he can hold it together until he goes home."

They were trying to figure out how to thank him. Then Standby asked, "What about the CO? Can you keep this from him?"

Top smiled again. "The CO is always informed, Troop."

He turned and put his hand on the doorknob. "Oh, and one more thing ..."

"Yeah?"

"Let's get the fucking Stratego game the hell out of the sound booth."

# Martin

A long-time birder with over 100 species on her life list, Sheri had an affinity for the Purple Martin, perhaps because the species shared the name of her best friend growing up. The martins' sweptback, pointed wings, the dark purple sheen of their plumage, and their alert, quick eyes matched the girl's slim, small frame, her sleek black hair, the bright interested look,

Or, having always had a desire to travel (seldom fulfilled), perhaps Sheri was drawn to (all) the [M]martins' heroic journeys—the birds flights from the north Amazon basin to eastern North Carolina and back, the girl's from southeast Missouri to Southeast Asia and …well back, but not as the same person who went. Still, survival skills.

Martin Fairchild was also "the girl who got away" from Alfred before he met and married Sheri. Both sorrowed when Martin got away from it all.

After the series of threats to the last bird— death by water, turtle, cat, owl, snake—Sheri was reminded of her friend's experience before the final downturn.

"It's just not fair," she lamented to her husband as they began the three-hour drive from the family's river house toward their home in central Virginia. "The beautiful moon, spectacular sunset, a drop in temperature so unlike August. All beautiful. And then ...predators!"

"It is the natural order, of course—sunrise, sunset; summer to fall; predator and prey. A nurse, you have to know about the cycle of life and death."

Alfred, the scientist, could be irritatingly matter-of-fact, as if logic and the laws of nature were so straightforward there could be no reason to rise up and complain about them.

"Oh, I agree," she sighed. "It's not just the little bird that's upset me. It's ...you know, Martin."

"Ah!" Alfred's sigh meant he knew she was returning to a series of events she'd been struggling with for decades. "The girl who got away,"

"Well, it starts with a near drowning, right?"

Their purple martins raised one or two broods in their April-August stay in the states. Over the past week she and Alfred had been watching the parents coax fledglings out of the house at the river's edge. The youngsters could begin hunting · on their own for mosquitos and other bugs over the water. One little bird seemed not up to the task, dipping down from the fifteen-foot-high house to bounce along the surface like a water skier about to cartwheel into the waves.

"Yes, you saved the bird, though, and Martin didn't face drowning, did she?"

"Well, yes and no. I might never have told you how much she feared the water." Sheri had had to coach her childhood friend through swim training, required for assignment to a medical facility in Vietnam.

Having grown up and gone to nursing school at the University of Missouri together, she and Sheri then worked in the same St. Louis hospital for three years. Roommates throughout, they became even faster friends as they took on the pediatric ward's medical and emotional challenges. Alfred was working in the hospital lab and, meeting Martin, asked her out several times.

Martin had tried every excuse she could to avoid the swimming test—inner ear problems, abdominal muscle weakness, even an exaggerated history of vaginal yeast infections. But she still had to jump into an Olympic sized pool, swim a length facedown, return on her back. And she wanted desperately to serve overseas as her mother had in World War II.

The one purple martin at the Fortunes' waterfront house who couldn't stay airborne ended up floundering against the bulkhead at the edge of their property. "I'm going to get her up onto land," she told Alfred and ran for his makeshift boat hook (an old broomstick with a coat hangar bent into a crooked U-shape and taped to the end).

They both knew large snapping turtles, famous in this area, swam beneath the river's surface and dragged down goslings, baby ducks, other small water fowl.

"You get your scent on that bird, and the parents will abandon it. Leave the guy alone. It's like the butterfly and the cocoon—they have to fight their way into life."

"Bullshit," Sheri said; but she did put on gloves. And she lifted the little martin out of the water. "She'll rest a bit, get her strength, join her brothers and sisters for the long journey south," she insisted.

Sheri's friend Martin had made the down lap swimming relatively comfortably, but she floundered near the end of the return lap. Gulping in water, coughing, frantically flailing her arms, she just managed to fling one hand as far the spill tray at the pool's edge. She had passed this test, not anticipating the much more difficult ones to come. Twice she ended up in Vietnamese waters. Both times she had to be rescued.

Alfred pulled Sheri out of her reveries by continuing the story of the bird. "It's a good thing we kept our eyes out for cats. Your little friend would have made a nice meal for the Jensens' two Siamese prowlers."

Sheri had watched the bird resting by the bulkhead for a few minutes. Then, reminded of the neighbors' pets, she decided to scoop her up again and put her on the bank close to the birdhouse, which was on the other side of their property. Perhaps the martin parents would bring her something to eat or encourage her to take flight

99

from the ground. Alfred advised they continue to take turns, sentries against cat attack.

One of Martin's letters from Vietnam had mentioned a species of cat little known to the Western world. And, at least in one case, they were dangerous.

When Martin asked a soldier what happened to his arm and shoulder, he claimed he had been mauled by an animal. "Biggest f— …uh, biggest damned cat I ever saw," he said as she cleaned the wounds. "Pardon my language, Miss. Anyway, the d- …the thing dropped out of the trees onto my shoulders. Never had a clue he was up there."

Later, asking one of the Vietnamese interpreters, Sheri learned the only possible cat of that size would be the clouded leopard. In his country, Bao explained, pet-sized cats ended up in stew pots. He'd never heard of an attack against humans but admitted that any animal, when cornered, will fight.

Martin wrote Sheri how, before this encounter, missing the Ozarks of her youth, she'd fantasized about taking a hike up into the mountains west of the base. Now she foresaw a Southeast Asian version of the American mountain lion on the look-out for innocent hikers like herself. "How ironic would that be?" she wrote. "Eaten by cats in a war zone!"

"Are we stopping for ice cream?" Sheri asked Albert as they approached Courtland, Virginia. The Dairy Queen there was a favorite stop to break up

100

the trip.

"Blizzard?" he smiled. "Take your mind off …depressing topics."

The peanut butter cups blended into soft ice cream did hold her attention for a time. Then, as some circling turkey buzzards passed across the setting sun ahead of them, she recalled the owl.

A week earlier, she and Alfred had stood on the deck watching the Super Moon rise on the night of bird rescue (the purple martin disappeared from the ground and they believed she'd returned to the house). The flat land of Tidewater allowed the evening rays to travel horizontally over the house and, like a gigantic spotlight, illuminate the water in front of them. When that celestial body is closest to the earth in its elliptical orbit, the harvest moon dominates the horizon at dusk.

Trying to steady her camera on the deck's rail, Sheri saw some black shape swoop down from the left to the martin house and attach itself to the structure. "What is that?" she asked, clutching Alfred's arm and pointing.

"I …I don't know. Hawk? Osprey? Eagle?"

By the time they roused themselves to action— whatever the thing was, it was clearly after the martins—the winged shadow dropped from the house and flew off in the direction it had come.

"Oh, snap!" Alfred reported later. "It was probably an owl. They hunt at night, you know. And it says here they will attack martin houses."

101

He was reading from his iPad.

"Let me see?" Sheri learned how an owl attaches itself with one foot, grasping the edge of a hole into the house. When a panicked martin tries to flee, he grabs it with the other foot. Sheri worried that her little bird—rescued from drowning, protected from cats—had been snatched on the night of the Super Moon. The contrast between beauty and destruction was too dramatic to dismiss from her thoughts.

In her assignment with the 18th Surgical Hospital in Quang Tri, Martin watched small aircraft fly in and out of the base at all hours of the day and night. Their ascents and descents were smooth, reassuring sights. The attack choppers, though, the cobras, looked like giant birds of prey.

Especially late in her tour, Martin said she wanted to view the mountains west of the base from the air (since she wasn't going to hike in those forests). "Week after week you see that range of hills up against the sky, the sun setting over them every night, and you just wonder what it's like out there." She got her chance with a medical team was needed up the coast.

She'd written before that she and several other nurses had visited the ancient city of Hue. So, Sheri was not surprised that her friend's adventurous spirit was taking her off the base more and more as she approached her "date of return from overseas service." Only when she been home for some months did Martin admit that she had witnessed a tragedy on a ride back from that one mission.

Approaching Quang Tri, the tail rotor on another chopper conked out. The pilot could keep the bird in the air, but wasn't able to control the direction of flight. He tried to bring it down in an open field. As Sheri and her crew watched, the helicopter twirled and spun back into a convoy coming down the hillside. Its long blades slashed into the dirt and the trucks, killing the crew and two soldiers on the ground.

"She got away from so much over there," Sheri said to Alfred, putting her empty Blizzard into the cup holder behind the front seats. "Who would have thought the danger she couldn't escape was here?"

"It did follow her home," Alfred pointed out. "And now that we know so much more about PTSD, we can trace the origin of what happened back to Vietnam."

Sheri knew that was true, but more and more she'd been rethinking Martin's behavior once she returned to the states. The signs of her distress were there, but Sheri hadn't known enough to connect the dots. Now she believes she should have.

She sighed. "I guess we ought to have known to guard against snakes, too."

Sheri read—again too late—that you can use a circle of tight screen at the base of a martin house's pole to block a snake's path. They would do that next year.

On the morning after the Super Moon, Alfred was getting ready to take out his 14-foot day sailer when, studying her martin house from the dock, Sheri called, "Look at the martins. They're flying all round the house but not lighting. Is this the whole colony getting ready to depart for the equator and beyond?"

There must have been twenty-five or thirty little black and purple birds circling the house. They were not feeding, but their characteristic chirping was constant. Every few seconds one would fly up to a little platform in front of the holes, hover with wings flapping, but then dip down and away.

Alfred looked at the scene. "Is there something on the pole? It's looks, I don't know, fatter or something."

They walked over to inspect and then backed away. Sheri said, "I don't know what kind it is, but that's a pretty good-sized snake climbing up to the house."

Alfred got his boathook from the dock, came back, and, holding it at full length, prized the snake from the pole. Sheri urged him to be careful: it could be a water moccasin. "It's a rat snake," he assured her. But she suspected he was saying that so she wouldn't worry.

"Just chase it away or something," she urged, a chill running up her back. She hated snakes and thought about the deadly ones in Vietnam.

Martin had treated a number of civilians over there bitten by cobras. Since the venomous snake hunts in cultivated fields for its food, many of their human victims are poor farmers or members of their family.

GI's had the protection of boots and heavy clothing. If bitten, in most cases they were treated quickly. Many liked to tell of encounters in which the M-16 was more effective than even the spitting cobras.

The nurses knew the snakes could be in their own compound, searching for the rats that lived off garbage. So they made plenty of noise approaching their cots, walking to the latrine, coming or going from the mess hall.

Alfred was able to push the North Carolina snake—rat or moccasin—into the water off the bulkhead and assumed it would look for easier prey in other areas. After he had his gear in the boat, however, and was checking the rigging, Sheri called. "There it is again! It's slithering toward the pole. God, he's huge!"

"You want me to kill it?" he asked, climbing up on the dock and coming around to stand beside her. Usually she asserted that animals have to do what they have to do—cats chase birds, dogs go after rabbits, foxes hunt chickens. We might want to discourage them, but not exterminate them.

"Kill it," she said and walked up to the house.

Not owning a gun, Alfred got his garden hoe and gave the snake several sharp chops. It writhed and coiled, falling back into the water. It was not dead, though, and was able to swim off. They concluded, whether fatally wounded or not, it would not return. And, so far as they knew, it did not.

"You were pretty firm about the death penalty back there, with the snake," Alfred mused as he drove, the route so familiar he didn't need to think about the turns he would make. Semi-retired now, the couple split their time between the two states. "A decision to terminate is not quite like you."

She looked out her window and the countryside, soy bean fields close to harvest, cotton following. "There are cases …"

"It's still the girl who got away, isn't it? Not the birds. Or not just the birds. It's the 'Snake in the Grass.'"

"I'm remembering the last time I saw Martin."

Worried about more cats, owls, and snakes, they had watched the birds more closely. After a day or two, the martins were out over the water but didn't seem to be going into or out of the house. At different times of the day birds skimmed along the river and the bank, catching insects. But they went up into the trees, not to their former home.

Alfred's research revealed that, if a colony is sufficiently threatened, the birds will abandon the site. Though they're more vulnerable to predators in the trees, they're safer than in a place where they can be trapped. Sometimes, if it's late in the season, they'll start the long migration to the southern hemisphere a bit early.

After another day, Sheri walked down to the house at dusk and stared up at the dark, circular doorways to the apartments. Alfred would take the house down in the middle of winter, clean it, and put it back up for the next season. But now was not that time.

On the back side, Sheri saw one little bird peeking out. She knew it was her martin, the one she had pulled from the water where turtles might have gotten her.

Convinced that her little friend had waited for her. Of course, she thought, the martin would need her rescuer's permission to leave! So, she whispered, "Go home."

The bird cocked her head this way and that, blinking. Sheri said, "You should move on now. Follow your natural instinct and fly away to some safe spot in another world."

The next morning, inspecting the house again, she saw no bird looking back at her. "Safe," she told herself.

Less than an hour from home, she admitted to Alfred, "I can't forget the last time I saw Martin, in her apartment down by the base. What a dump she was living in!"

After she came back from Southeast Asia,

Martin left the Army and moved to the little town next to Fort Leonard Wood, though she had no job there. She was following a soldier she'd met overseas, a man Sheri did not like the moment she was introduced to him. She felt he had a mean look and nicknamed him "Snake in the Grass."

Alone with Sheri when he stepped out for a smoke, Martin giggled that he talked a lot about his "snake." "It's not a pet," she said, nudging Sheri's arm.

"You sure about this?" Sheri asked her friend before leaving. Martin seemed to her thinner and—despite the tropical sun—paler than she'd been before she left. She saw empty beer cans spilling out from the kitchen trashcan.

"He's the one." Martin shifted in her chair, and Sheri thought a flicker of pain crossed her face. "Of course, he has ...of course, he's adjusting to being back in the World. It's hard for them, you know. All they've seen, what they had to do."

Sheri studied her. "Yeah, I guess."

"They've been where there are no rules, just instincts, survival of the fittest. You know, it's a jungle—literally."

"Well, if you need anything ...if you decide you want to visit us in Columbia, just call. Or come on without calling."

"He'll be discharged in a month. We're going to start a new life together down in New Orleans. He has some buddies there who are opening a bar."

108

That wasn't the last time Sheri saw her friend. A few weeks later, she received several phone calls where no one spoke. She could hear breathing, but no words. Intuition said it was Martin, and she told Alfred she had to drive down to see about her.

There was no answer to Sheri's knocks on her door, but Martin's car was parked out front. Sheri told the apartment manager that she was Martin's sister and that she had called saying she was sick. Having rented to all sorts, he nodded knowingly and opened the door. They found her curled up on the floor of the small pantry, her eyes wild.

"Come with me," Sheri said, kneeling down and seeing bruises on one arm and below her neck.

Martin let Sheri take her to the hospital but refused to go back to Columbia with her. "I'm fine," she said. "I just had a little fall in the kitchen, got sort of disoriented."

Once she had been treated, the hospital wouldn't keep her without her consent. Back at the apartment complex, as Sheri was talking on the phone to Alfred, Martin got away. Sheri saw the car pulling into the street and speeding south.

After a week not hearing from Martin, Sheri contacted the Fairchild family in Sikeston. They weren't sure where she had gone. They hadn't known about the man Sheri had met.

Over the next few years, Sheri learned that the parents received post cards from various places— Louisiana, Mexico, Costa Rica—none with a return address. Martin always wrote that she was fine, "seeing the world."

Forty years later, Sheri still hoped to get a card herself. Or one day, she thought, she'd open the door and find her friend on the porch smiling in front of her.

"I like your version of the future," Alfred said, as they made the last turn headed into town.

Sheri had fantasized that one summer she would be sailing down the river, and the weather would turn rough. Sudden wind, dark clouds, then gusty rain. Unable to see landmarks, she would trim the sail, hope to spot what was ahead before colliding into it.

Then a tiny bird, a purple martin, would appear before her, flitting this way, that. She was, Sheri realized, pointing, a guide to safety.

It would be her martin, of course, the one who got away. She had returned from the Amazon one more time and was keeping an eye on the woman who had fought against the laws of nature. Together they would find safe harbor.

# Runaway Truck Ramp

Except for the twelve months in Vietnam, Norman Bench had lived all of his sixty-some years (including one at Fort Leonard Wood) in the Missouri Ozarks and had never seen a "runaway truck ramp." Driving through the Appalachians, though, on old Highway 60 in the fall of 2001, he saw his first and marveled at the simplicity of the idea and the necessity of its existence. Why didn't he see them in the step rises and falls of the long ridges where'd he grown up? Surely Show-me state residents had their own runaway trucks?

What Norm saw at the end of a long winding stretch of highway coming from the top of a Virginia mountain was simply a gravel ramp that went off to the right, down a final dip, and then up an incline. It came after a number of signs alerting drivers: "Runaway Truck Ramp 3 miles," then "2 miles," then "1 mile." He supposed the gravel was so deep in that path that a truck racing into it—its brakes having failed—would be like a man trying to run into the ocean. You'd churn to a halt and fall on your face. But that rapid deceleration would be much better than slamming into a series of tree trunks or a rock cliff.

Because no such thing would be needed in the flat coastal counties of eastern North Carolina, Norman didn't associate this highway safety feature with his friend Phillip's sad history. But then when he heard the last time from his late friend's daughter, a connection became clear.

"We found a will of sorts, or his journal," Linda told Norm over the phone. "It's kind of a rambling letter to us all. But he talks a lot about you, how much he valued your friendship."

"We tried to stay in touch, but his being in North Carolina and me out here, it was hard." Norman had always felt guilty that he had visited Phil only once in twenty years and even sometimes resented the endless phone conversations he had to endure with his friend. He'd even deliberately not included a second visit to Tidewater when he took his wife to see the Shenandoah valley.

"I know," Linda admitted. "Jim and I couldn't even come down from DC as much as we wanted during the years our children were little. Daddy felt lonely even when Mother was alive. Once or twice a year we'd be there. But we couldn't see that much difference. And, of course, for so many years Mother hid everything from us."

Norman had suspected the drinking, but not, until near the end, the other things. Even now he didn't want to remember.

He and Phil had served in the same signal corps unit in Vietnam's I Corps, but they had much different tasks to perform. Norm was in "Base Ops," installing and maintaining communication systems for 1st Brigade, 5th Infantry Division in Quang Tri. His friend was sent out to more remote

112

places to adjust equipment, train operators, install new technology. Phil was a native of the state that said it was "First in Flight," but he claimed that shouldn't mean he was put on every wandering helicopter headed out to nowhere.

Growing up and working hard on a farm in North Carolina, he had to walk or hitch rides to school. Losing his father at age twelve meant he had no chance of going to college, so he enlisted to learn, he thought, the telephone trade. He joked that he got his "bell rung pretty good in Vietnam" but returned to work for Ma Bell for over twenty years.

During the same period Norman, who, when he was drafted, was four years older and already had a degree in electrical engineering, established his own company, Stable, Inc. Getting financial help from two WWII veterans in the local bank, he developed, installed, and maintained electronic sensing equipment that monitored home appliances from furnaces to exhaust fans. Any hint of malfunction or unusual performance was recorded and sent back to the company office so that repair or replacement could be planned. He claimed he caught trouble early, before a system went into rapid decline and collapse.

Norman felt that his steady rise in a profession was accentuated by stumbling blocks in his friend's slow-moving career. "Hey, good buddy," Phil might say in a late-night phone call. "What's going on out there in …is it Arkansas or Oklahoma?"

113

"It's Missouri, Phil, and you damn well know it. Things are good, just busy. What's up with you?"

"Samo, samo, my friend. I get more in debt each year. Maggie wants a new dress, the car needs tires, children have to have something for Christmas. You know how it is."

Norm didn't. He managed the family budget as relentlessly as his company's finances. Except for the original mortgage on the office and warehouse, Stable's business "debits" never outran "credits." Even he wasn't sure why he was so meticulous, but the benefits were increasingly evident in his children's college funds, a retirement investment account, an emergency fund.

"Aren't you getting raises from the telephone company? That should help."

"Too little, too slow, sometimes not at all. They're some guys younger than me getting ahead in the company. These college kids don't want to be out on the line first, and the bosses let them skip that phase."

Norman knew that, because of his military experience, Phil was thought most prepared for the toughest assignments: in the cypress swamps, wherever rivers flooded annually, after a hurricane took the tops off pines. The company seemed malicious in scheduling these jobs as part of his regular shifts so that he didn't get paid overtime.

"Have you thought about going to school at night? Using the GI Bill to catch up with the guys

114

who stayed home?"

Norman had done that himself, earned an M.S. at Southeast Missouri State that he didn't need for his work but that impressed potential clients. Sarah taught kindergarten, so, while he worked and took classes, she had time to take the kids (a son and a daughter, deliberately spaced three years apart) to school and meet them at home. She encouraged Norm in every venture, joking that his "graduate student" status made him young again—and sexy.

"Man, I can't be in a classroom with eighteen-year-olds still tied to their Momma's apron. I sat in on a beginning course once, and the girls—man, they don't wear *any* clothes! They're a frickin' distraction. No, I've gotten into the backwater. I'll just have to stick it out so long as I can still go fishin' most weekends."

He had a simple john boat, passed down from his father-in-law, with a five horsepower engine. He could drift along the shore of the Chowan River and up the little creeks that fed it casting for bass, trout, flounder. In the good years he put out crab pots, and Maggie froze meat for the winters. The family needed what he could catch when times were bad. And they were more often bad than good.

Norm wondered now and then if it had been fair he had the better assignment in Vietnam, spending nearly all of his year on the base. He became involved designing ways to combat the challenge of Vietnam's varied landscape that paid

115

off later in his civilian life. Steep mountains, dense jungles, jagged coasts, and winding rivers made communication from region to region difficult. And rapid, efficient transportation of troops and support was vital to (what they believed at the time was) the continuing success of the mission.

Norman helped develop the technology of "troposcatter," bouncing radio signals off the atmosphere and back to earth and thus bypassing terrain that blocked older methods of transmission. It was as if they had found a way to level out the landscape, so coordination of different units improved dramatically. Forces were moved to necessary locations faster, countering enemy assaults and staging surprise allied forays.

"How do I get on your team?" Phil asked Norm at the E-4 club one night early in their tour. A five-person Philippine band had been flown in for shows on consecutive nights. They played American rock 'n' roll—badly.

"It's up to the CO, I guess. I don't even know how *I* got this assignment." He suspected, though, that his college degree put him several steps ahead of Phil. "Why don't you talk to him?"

"Ah, shit. I know guys like Lancaster. Not only does he think I'm stupid, he can tell I'm from the South. Dumb redneck is all he sees."

Phil's accent was pronounced; and out of pride he refused to alter it. Sometimes he even laid it on. When he was asked out at a firebase to fix a radio, he might say in his most pronounced Southern

116

drawl, "Well, now, I don't rightly know how to read this 'ere manual 'cause my school teacher — she was married to her cousin who drank a bit too much of our moonshine and their kids was morons — and getting to school without no shoes and only dirt roads warn't easy — but I'll see what I can do."

From the stage, Norman heard the Philippine vocalist, wailing, "*And I wonder — I wah-wah-wah-wah-wonder, / Why, Why, why, why, why, why she ran away.*" Like many G.I.'s, he wanted to run away himself.

Those who knew Phil came to realize he was better at diagnosing and repairing equipment than most of the men; but officers, on six-month rotations, didn't have time — and often didn't want to take time — to get to know their personnel. And Phil would go on binges from time to time, barely able to function when he returned to duty or even ending up in sickbay to dry out. So he kept being "volunteered" to travel out to firebases and run cable or patch up radios with bullet holes in them. And there was that time the chopper nearly went down.

Norman drove down to see Phil one time, after a business trip to North Carolina's Research Triangle. He tried not to notice the disarray in his friend's doublewide, which sat on a half-acre lot without trees. "Maggie inherited the land from her Daddy," Phil explained. "And we used to have a pretty nice garden out back."

Norman could see that the corn was stunted, the tomato plants were pulling loose from their stakes, and there were weeds between the rows. "Hasn't done so well the last few years. Daddy says we need to plant some different crops, ..." Maggie's voice trailed off.

His friend was drifting, Norm realized, and the current of more children (there were three now, Linda the youngest), occasional illnesses, and poor money management were taking him away from stability.

"You ever think of moving, starting over somewhere else?" Norm asked him, thinking vaguely that he could use Phil's skills in his own business.

"Couldn't leave this area, not me or Maggie. What family we got left is all close by, and no place else is like this." He waved an arm in front of him, downed another beer, and squeezed the can flat. "I saw some of the rest of the world, you know — back in the war. I didn't think much of it and came back to North Carolina to live whatever time I have left here."

Norman sipped his beer. "I can see that. I like River County, where I live, for the same reasons. I've been there most of my life. But, you know, down where we are, the Bootheel, the country's not that different from around here. Flat river bottom farms, swamps, not too crowded. There might be opportunities for you."

Phil stood up and shook Norm's hand. "Damn

118

if you ain't a good friend! I might could work for you. But even if it is flat country, it's a damn thousand miles away. And so you've got rivers, but I need to see the ocean now and again."

Norman left it at that, but later made the same offer several times by telephone. Phil always brushed him off, claiming things were picking up for him. Norm wished he could talk to Maggie, but she always passed the phone to her husband or, if he wasn't there, hung up quickly. It saddened him to realize she felt awkward talking to someone she felt was far above her family's status.

Norman knew his own success had its price: despite insisting on regularly spending time with his family, he forsook vacations and holidays to manage Stable. Unwilling to turn control over to even his experienced and qualified managers, he limited the company's scope, size, and clientele. He would stay small and one day pass the company on to one of his children or the employees themselves.

The call before the last from North Carolina worried him. "Hey, let me ask you something, Norm," Phil said. "You still okay with heights? I mean getting up on rooftops to check air handlers or maybe inspect the pipes and wires on the outside walls."

"Now that you mention it, it isn't as easy as it used to be. I'm a bit the same way about small spaces. I guess it comes with age. Fortunately, I've got young guys to do it for me." He regretted it as soon as he'd said it.

119

"Used to be I could go up a pole, never think about it. Now, if I look down, the ground can come rushing up at me. And top of a power station or something, there's that impulse to jump. Have to stay back from the edge. Maggie says I need to get out of the field, work in the office after all these years."

"Makes sense to me. You've earned it."

There was a pause, and Norman thought he could hear his friend take a long drink, let out air afterwards. "Yeah, well, tell that to Ma Bell. The big boys aren't offering me much. They say I'm too good out where the goin' gets tough. Shit. They just don't want me around the office."

"What about changing companies? There are a lot of competitors now. Somebody should be willing to pay for your experience."

There was a long pause. "Sometimes I dream, man, that I'm back there." He didn't have to say where. "That bird in a tailspin."

Norm had heard about it afterwards from the helicopter gunner. A Huey had a safety procedure called "autorotation." In the case of engine failure, the pilot disconnects the main rotor blades from the engine, allowing them to be turned by the air through which the helicopter is descending. Resistance slows the fall. And because the tail rotor is connected to the main rotor, those blades continue to turn and the pilot can steer …in ideal conditions.

120

The chopper Phil was on was hit by ground fire leaving the area of a mountain top recon base. The steep slopes ahead of them meant there was nowhere close to land, but, if the pilot could keep control, he could descend on a path parallel to the mountainside. The crew stayed calm, but Phil panicked.

He had never been comfortable flying and did all he could to avoid riding on small planes or the big C-30 cargo carriers, but he'd convinced himself that autorotation would save him from any helicopter crash. He could never say how far the bird dropped or how long the ride was, but he admitted to the loss of bowel control common in such situations.

Back at Quang Tri he laughed about his adventure. And his buddies felt he had been lucky: he had a war story to tell but had suffered no injury. Every trip after that was preceded and followed by heavy drinking. The universal fear — dying the day before you were to go home — intensified the shorter his remaining time became. He admitted to Norm that he even fantasized his Freedom Bird would go down in some freak tropical storm.

Years later, when Norm thought about the last phone conversation he had with Phil, he suspected a deeper sorrow was coming out.

Norman had been reading that, after more American wars, the medical profession and society at large were starting to understand PTSD as a condition consciously or unconsciously masked by veterans. Especially in his generation, few returning soldiers wanted to admit to or share their nightmares. But decades after the experience the flashbacks can increase in frequency and intensity. It's a downward spiral, usually treated with alcohol and drugs that only accelerate the collapse.

Before Norm could decide what, if anything, to do for his friend, he got the last call, this time from Maggie. "His truck went into the river," she said. "He was probably dead from hitting the water. I'm just glad he wasn't trapped in there."

"Oh, my God! I'm so sorry. Did he lose control? Was it bad weather? What the hell happened?"

"They'd been working on a new bridge. He was coming back from a job; it was dark. He must not have seen the signs."

"Well, this is such a shock. When's the service. I'll try to come."

"Oh, we done that already. And it was simple, just family and a few friends."

He tried to organize his thoughts. "But what can I do to help you? Are you okay ...uh ...financially?"

"Oh, yeah. I'll get his pension from the phone company." She paused. "I have my church, and one of the boys lives just an hour away."

She didn't sound okay, but Norm didn't know what to do. It was so sudden. So final. But there had been signs he had ignored.

Later, he got one of his younger employees to go on the internet and find out what had happened. The highway department had left the old bridge standing while they built a new one parallel to it. For a time, northbound traffic was on one lane of the old bridge, southbound on one lane of the new. When both lanes of the new bridge were finally opened, they began bringing down the old bridge section by section. The final part, the one closest to shore, was to be dismantled last. It rose steeply from the ground to provide clearance for boat traffic in the middle of the river. The night Phil died, the old road still extended from the bank about fifty feet out over the water.

Even though barricades were in place to send traffic to the new section of road, which slanted off toward the new bridge, Phil went right through them. His truck went over the end of the old bridge and dove into the water, at that point less than four feet deep. As Maggie had said, according to the coroner, he died instantly when his head hit the windshield on impact.

It was harder for Norm's junior associate to find the official highway patrol report, but the investigation did not show alcohol in Phil's system. Though he was driving too fast, maybe—according to tire tracks —even accelerating, he was stone cold sober when he hit the water.

The daughter, Linda, filled in the blanks. "He started using drugs," she told Norman. "First it was marijuana. He'd read it helped with pain. And his back hurt real bad after all those years of climbing poles, going into crawl spaces, digging up cable."

"I know some doctors are prescribing it, but I guess he had to get his own?"

"Yes. And that's how it got worse. Whoever he was buying from got him into pills, crack, meth. He was a tailspin, but no one recognized the signs."

Norm could imagine it. Frustration at work, nightmares, his body deteriorating. And the relief would have been mental as well as physical. "You don't think," he asked her, "You don't think he knew what he was doing when he drove off that bridge?"

She sighed. "We'll never know. And, of course, I wouldn't want anything to lead to an inquiry at this point—the insurance company, Ma Bell." She paused. "That's why ...that's why I burned his journal. Let him rest in peace."

"Amen," agreed Norm, but he didn't feel at peace himself. His own security seemed unearned, and so did Phil's fall into oblivion. It was as if both trajectories had been determined the day they arrived together in Quang Tri—or even earlier. He had been routed toward salvation, and Phil was charted to hell. One path went up, the other went down. Who or what had set them on their courses? And why the hell was there no runaway truck ramp for his friend?

# Blood Drive

Even after thirty years, Peter Banks still remembered some of the slightly risqué radio announcements for the blood drive: "Come in and let me hold your ...[provocative pause] ...hand." The sultry voice seeking male donors in the Fort Campbell, Kentucky, area belonged to Major Torente's attractive wife.

Specialist Banks couldn't get used to the double entendre announcements then, even though he was the one ordered by the CO to compose them. Now, however, he saw it all as symptomatic of the nation's painful transition from one era to another.

"'Lay across my big brass bed,'" crooned Delmara, her husky voice not that different from Bob Dylan's. Peter flinched as her red lips licked the large microphone in the sound booth. "It'll only take you twenty minutes ...to finish."

Then Peter broke in to give the details. "Yes, we need your blood, soldier." His Midwestern speech patterns were thought standard in those days before accents were understood to assert cultural identity; and he'd worked hard to develop a rich announcer's voice. "The supply for our troops in Vietnam is low," he continued. "And Fort Campbell's Commander, General Rivers, has promised we'll pitch in and contribute our share."

Until recently, blood for the military in Vietnam had been supplied by donations collected in Japan, Korea, and Okinawa. But shortfalls had led to frequent stateside drives. Peter had read that bleeding to death accounted for something like 50% of battlefield casualties. Until now he worried only about the death part, not the process of dying.

Mrs. Torente had to lean to one side on her stool for Peter to reach the microphone; and she didn't leave him quite enough room to do his part. Maybe invading his space was just an aspect of her outgoing, flirtatious personality; but it seemed to him—a young man far behind the sexual revolution's forefront—like improper fraternization between ranks, sexes, and generations. He had no idea of her culture's different approach to space.

"All you need to do is relax, Troop; and I'll do the rest."

"Relax yo' ass, and it'll be in the 'Nam," sniped Specialist Jason Ford, editing the tape while Mrs. Torente took a coffee break. According to Jason, the people of his race tended to end up in the field a lot more often than the white guys. He asserted that half of base personnel were black, though Peter had found data that contradicted those number.

"Let's just get this done," Peter told Jason. He'd never met a black person until he went to college, and he didn't understand race. Naive, he still thought it was possible to see and treat everyone as equal. After all, wasn't that why they were in Southeast Asia, to promote democracy?

126

Delmara wooed her listeners with a delivery that never revealed her ethnicity. "I might make you light-headed, soldier, but it'll be worth it." She had had experience as a television weather girl before she married. The mother of three, one almost as old as Peter, she had still kept her figure. The men in the office noticed.

Peter had become fatalistic about the future since the chopper his friend Jimmy Poole was on took a nose dive into a rice patty in the Mekong Delta. But he still fretted that the blood drive project, several hours behind schedule, would be further delayed, costing him his weekend leave.

"Food for the leeches, like too many of my buddies," Jason had said of Jimmy. He'd never known Pete's friend. "I've seen it a hundred times." He'd survived his tour and seldom missed a chance to scare those who hadn't—especially the white guys. Peter concluded that the only category you were in that mattered over there was lucky.

It wasn't just the prospect of cancelled leave that irritated Peter; it was more evidence of his complete loss of control. The "U.S. of Army" had possession of his very body. Caught in a system that swept him wherever it wanted him to go, he could not identify the location he would be in the next five minutes, the next three weeks, the next (to be exact) 415 days (and a wake-up).

For weeks he'd been fantasizing a weekend on leave, out of reach of reveille and telephone alert. He would float the Cumberland River from

Clarksville to the River Bend National Wildlife Refuge, a six-pack of beer melting ice in the canoe with him, his own carefully crafted, shad-imitating lures trailing in his wake. Now he feared he would be anchored to his stool in the control booth.

"The Man needs to get him a sister in here," observed Jason. "My half of the base ain't listening to this shit."

Her liquid voice oozing down the wire to his headset mesmerized Peter. But maybe, he thought, blacks, hearing Mrs. Torente—who sounded white—would reserve their blood for drives sponsored by their own churches. What did he know?

He did remember a white guy from South Carolina whispering to him in basic training—as they were getting their blood typed—that he'd never take a "nigger's" blood. "You pass it on, man. Your children get it, and two or three generations down the line the family's ruined." Would this idiot truly rather watch his blood sink into the dirt if he were wounded in combat? Banks believed that blood is blood; it has no race.

Still, he understood how groups band together. At the prestigious East Coast university he had attended for a year anti-war protesters staged a blood drive. Students and faculty were urged to give blood to show their commitment to life and peace. The pints went to the university's own medical facilities; and Peter saw that the donors were part of a private system which they had chosen to join. Their own blood circulated back to nourish themselves and their friends.

It was also true that his mother had been appalled when one of her nephews married a Japanese woman. A quarter of a century earlier, Mrs. Banks' cousin had died on the Bataan Death March. "And now," she told her son, "I'll have half-breeds in my family." For her, the "Yellow Peril" was real.

Still, Major Torente's advertising campaign—dubbed in the office "The Mother Sucker of all Blood Drives"—proved remarkably successful: more pints in two days than any campaign of the last five years. The program's place in the larger course of history wasn't clear to Peter, however, until decades later when he heard a recording of Bob Dylan singing "Lay, lady, lay, across my big brass bed" and waxed nostalgic.

A song that had been thought too explicit in its sexuality was tame by today's standards; and the radical, anti-war singer had become a popular icon. It made Peter wonder if he and his fellow baby-boomers had gone soft with age. While the division between warriors and protesters remained bitter for some on both sides, to him the two groups had merged into the stream of history, a single era of sorrow and loss, anger and resentment, injury and healing.

He knew he had been lucky over there; but, still, he had lost friends, one of them black. And a current co-worker, who'd been exposed to Agent

Orange, was dying of a cancer associated with that herbicide. Fighting the war all over again, thought Peter, wouldn't change the diagnosis. Better to help by transporting Joseph to and from his chemo sessions, holding his wife's hand as they waited.

He chuckled to himself when he finally checked the organ donor box on his driver's license. Still, he felt light-headed whenever he contemplated his kidney one day filtering another person's blood. It was not that we were all identical, he concluded, but the same blood drives us all forward.

# The Death of Short-timer Sam

"Of course, I knew Johnny," said Greg. "He's the guy who killed Short-timer Sam."

Jeff asked, "Killed him? As in murdered?"

Mark laughed. "No, as in 'put the quietus on' the radio show. A day in March—maybe the Ides of ..., in fact—Johnny pushed the brass too far, and they canceled the program." His smile faded as he remembered the day *after* they killed Short-timer Sam, the radio personality. That was when the voice of Sam was snuffed out. That is, Johnny died.

"You'd better explain" said Cathy. "Us aging spouses of aging vets are out of the loop again and wondering which of you did what to whom."

Recently, she and Ann had found their husbands talking more about their long-ago service than they ever had. And, reading about the struggles of the next generation of veterans, they were willing to listen.

Mark and Jeff had been drafted forty years earlier and did tours in Vietnam, though they didn't know each other at the time. Jeff had grown up in Philadelphia, Mark in Fairfield, Missouri; so they entered the service in different states through Fort Dix and Fort Leonard Wood. They met six years later when they were both hired by the same university. For a long time they never talked about

131

their experiences, but recently they'd opened up to each other. Still, they told their wives very little.

"I was an 'information specialist,'" explained Mark to Ann and Cathy, "a reporter assigned to USARV-HQ—um, that's Army headquarters in Vietnam. My group produced broadcast announcements from the giant concrete complex in Long Binh. We used to joke that it would become 'Hanoi South' one day. Anyway, we had a pretty good sound studio, big ten-inch tape decks, first class microphones. The finished products went out on Armed Services Radio."

Jeff added. "And where I was—out on the coast in Nha Trang—I heard these nameless voices droning over the airways about security, providing sanitized battle summaries, reminding us of procedures and opportunities. And just about a month ago I found that one of those voices belonged to a man I've worked with for over thirty years."

"The same man who filled your ear with advice and complaints all the time you were department chair," laughed Mark. "And let me admit, you have always been a good listener."

Until their retirements last month, the two men had been colleagues at South Central Missouri State University in Fairfield, a small city bisected by Historic Route 66. Jeff had been department chair for nearly a decade.

Cathy frowned. "He's a good listener for anyone but his wife."

"Now you're picking on the hard-of-hearing." Jeff knew he needed hearing aides but kept putting off the tiresome project of weighing options and making choices. "And it may be you're hard-of-speaking."

Ann said, "I think you're suffering from a couple's condition, especially the long-of-married ones. Each spouse has a voice that can't reach the other even when you're in the same room. Oh, we know about that one!"

The two couples had taken the 90-minute drive into St. Louis to celebrate their retirements by seeing a Cardinals game and going out to dinner.

Mark held up a hand. "I've promised to work on it—both paying attention and finding out about hearing aides. But it is also an age thing. All those rock music concerts have deafened our generation."

Jeff turned to his wife. "Getting back to the subject, did you know that you could take college courses while over there? Career advancement for lifers. 'Lifers.' by the way, are career military."

"But you both already had your degrees, right?" Cathy pointed out.

"Yes," Mark said, "we received our diplomas and our 'Greetings' from Uncle Sam the same summer, but Jeff was at Washington Lee in Virginia and I was here at Washington University."

Jeff added, "I ended up in Military Intelligence, gathering and interpreting data about enemy operations in our region while Mark was providing

133

information concerning what goes on inside the U.S. of Army."

"That needs explanation to those already in uniform?"

"Oh, how naive the sweet sex!" laughed Jeff. "And you a career teacher, too, who has survived scores of empty education workshops. Yes, they have to tell us how to blouse our fatigues in the morning and then tell us again, either because they assume we're not paying attention or that whatever they say goes in one ear and out the other."

Mark put down the menu he'd been studying and said, "Let me tell you about Johnny, the voice of Short-timer Sam, a would-be draft dodger who caved at the last moment. He'd bought a plane ticket to Vancouver, was in touch with ex-patriots there, and had said goodbye to all his friends at Princeton. He was going to be a spokesperson for the anti-war movement in Canada. But, at the last minute, he realized he just couldn't do that to his parents back in Texas."

"A good number of men did," observed Jeff. "Some say as many as 50,000—oddly close to the number that were KIA in Vietnam." There was no need to explain that acronym.

"Johnny called his parents the night before his flight to give them the news, but when he got close to saying he was leaving the country, his throat tightened and the words wouldn't come out. 'To hell with it,' he told his friends and went down to the Selective Service Office the next morning."

Ann frowned. "This doesn't sound like a story with a happy ending, and we're here to enjoy ourselves. Maybe it's time for a refill." She twisted her wine glass around by the stem.

Cathy looked at her intensely. "I kind of agree, but it's also time we heard some stories from these men's tours." She signaled their server at Pujols Restaurant. "But if you're ready, we can put in our orders."

Both women had married several years after the men returned from Vietnam. Fellow sociology majors at Drury College in Springfield, they became co-workers at the Social Security office in Fairfield and specialized in interviewing country people who needed help understanding and filling out government forms.

Ann and Cathy had been friends before their future husbands were hired at the university. After the weddings—a year apart—the two couples bought homes in the same neighborhood, their children grew up together, they went to the same church. Vietnam, however, was a giant blank space in their collective memory, those stories locked up in a soundproof room.

"Anyway," Mark went on after their server departed, "Short-timer Sam was a made-up character, first having a column in *Stars and Stripes*, then appearing regularly on the radio. He served as an advice columnist for active duty soldiers, kind of like *Dear Abbey.*"

"Ah, a version of Uncle Sam, then, but after

you'd received your 'greetings.'"

"Right! He answered questions on how to send money to your family back home, who to see if you wanted to extend your tour, why you shouldn't sleep with mama-san—the woman who cleaned our hootch—uh, barracks."

"'Extend your tour'? Surely, all you needed guidance on was how to get out of there as quickly as possible. All I've ever heard about that war was how everyone wanted to come home."

"True. But before you could get on a 'Freedom Bird'—the plane that would take you back to The World—you had to become a 'short-timer,' that is, someone who is approaching his DEROS."

"'Date of Expected Release from Overseas Service,'" explained Jeff. "Oh, I remember my short-timer stick! You whittled off a bit each day with the idea that there was only a toothpick to hand to your turtle—your replacement."

"You also passed on wisdom because you were a clever old fellow, having survived your tour. A short-timer—Short-timer Sam—had advice to offer in print and on the air."

Jeff grinned, "Ah, the short-timer sayings: 'I'm so short I can't see the lawn for the grass,' 'I'm so short a bug's ass is eye level,' 'I'm so short I have to use a snorkel to get across a rain puddle.'"

"Those, of course, are some of the clean ones. The favorite image for a short-timer was a helmet resting on two boots, a hand somehow coming

136

around to salute."

"And you went through stages of shortness. Everyone started at 365 days ...well, 364 and 'a wake-up.' But eventually you could say 'I'm under a hundred,' then 'a two-digit midget,' finally 'a zero-hero.'"

"But get back to what happened to Short-timer Sam," Ann insisted. "That is, to Johnny."

Mark sighed, reached for his second beer as the server took away his empty glass and set down a second round of appetizers. "Johnny loved being Short-timer Sam. Back in 'The World,' — the States — he was studying to be a sports announcer. Harry Carey — the voice of the Cardinals when we were growing up, then the A's, the White Sox, the Cubs — was his hero."

Jeff remembered, "'Holy Cow, that might be outta' here!' — that was his famous call heard by fans in St. Louis, Oakland, Chicago."

Cathy said, "So, being on the radio over there was great experience that would have helped him after he was a civilian again. Surely he didn't spoil his own nest?"

"I'm afraid he did. But he was driven by certain demons. We all are, of course, but his resentment of the war and getting drafted got the better of him. Maybe it was also his inability to tell his parents the truth about his feelings."

Jeff reached for the spinach dip. "Mark and I were among the lucky ones — came home, settled

137

our demons, went to graduate school on the GI Bill ...well, we were *helped* by the GI Bill."

"Right. It didn't cover everything, as it did for the WWII vets. But we got through, got jobs, met wonderful women, and the rest is history."

"Oh, brother!" said both women.

"Well," Mark continued, "let me tell you about the last broadcast of Short-timer Sam. It explained how to get the University of Maryland to accept your military experience as coursework toward a college degree."

Jeff said, "Ah, yes, targeting air strikes would be geography, PSYOPs would be—well, psychology—and launching mortars would be physics. I figure most of the grunts would come out of there with at least an associate's degree. Well, assuming they got out of there at all ..."

"It was a little better than that," Mark said, "but the university's extension office did want to have men make progress, so they concluded that some military training matched courses in civilian education. And, by the way, the faculty weren't so popular back home for helping the military. There were protests, angry voices on campus. And the professors who volunteered were not always as safe as we told them they'd be."

Ann was eyeing her husband closely. "You've always claimed your job wasn't dangerous."

"We were in a well-fortified base, the war was winding down ...or so we were told."

"Didn't you leave the base on story assignments?"

"Yeah, but they didn't send me into hot spots. My job was to show how well the Vietnamese were doing taking over control of the country's infrastructure, making it possible for the Americans to leave. Those stories were heard back in the states. So, anyway, yes, I did do field work as well as studio work, but I stayed out of danger."

Jeff added. "Nha Trang was a big base, too, but now and then we did get rockets, very rarely mortars, when I was there. You had to be very unlucky to get wasted — get killed."

"Didn't some men die from illness or accidents?"

"'Non-combat casualties'? Sure. That's how Johnny's demise was recorded. And don't forget deaths from 'friendly fire' — our own and ARVN's. That's the Army of the Republic of Vietnam, the military of a country that no longer exists. Most civilians don't know how to read casualty reports and assume all deaths are KIAs. Ah, here come our entrees."

Once their dishes were arranged and the server had added cheese as desired, Mark went on. "You see, Johnny was a large man, big body, big voice. And he loved to eat. He saw coming to Southeast Asia as an opportunity to sample exotic foods — fertilized duck egg, silk worm dishes, paddy snails, bull penis, even dog, which they do cook there."

"Maybe we'd better wait until the coffee to talk about such things. I want to enjoy this all-American T-bone and an Idaho baked potato."

"Hmm. I hear you. Well, his last show wasn't about eating weird stuff. But it not only had the double entendres he'd been slipping into recent broadcasts, but also indirect anti-war material. 'Want to fulfill your college history requirement? Take Western Civilization and hear thrilling lectures on how the French fared just down the road at Dien Bein Phu.'"

"That's the battle that drove them out of the colonial business, isn't it?

"Correct. It left a vacuum into which America was sucked. Let's see, there was something about languages, too. 'Get credits toward your degree by learning how to say 'Where is the bathroom?' in Japanese. You might be a professional translator, but you'll also be an expert in kamikaze preparation."

"Seriously? He said that?"

"Well, something close to that. And he talked fast, so a lot of stuff got past the brass, who weren't listening carefully ...until near the end. I guess they knew the show was short before we did."

"Wasn't there something about chemistry?" asked Jeff.

"Oh, yeah. 'Not only can you satisfy your science requirement, you'll be able to identify the good plants from the weed, which can help you while you're in-country as well as back in the The World.'"

"Marijuana was the drug of choice over there," Jeff confirmed, "though there was plenty of American beer in all the enlisted men's clubs."

Ann tilted her head back and gave a sly smile. "Go back to the racy stuff Johnny inserted — if I can use that word — into his Short-timer Sam programs."

"It was something just like that — ordinary words or phrases that have other meanings in different contexts: 'shaft,' 'going down,' 'getting some.' And it was the way he said it, pausing to make you notice those words."

Cathy laughed. "Now I'm wondering what the two of you …inserted …into your lectures all these years! It's probably a miracle charges weren't brought against you."

Mark shook his head. "Oh, we've always been most proper. Especially in recent years, with political correctness, you have to be very careful about what you say and how it might be misunderstood by students who have an entirely different culture."

Ann said, "Well, after you finally figured out your retirement options as presented in official state policy, I don't want to hear that some bureaucratic official is re-examining your pension based on a belated student complaint." Both men had struggled with the institutional double-talk concerning health insurance options, survivor benefits, methods of payment.

"Agreed." Mark paused to let the server clear the dishes and for everyone to review the dessert menu. Then he continued. "Johnny didn't get to his retirement, of course, And his family didn't receive the death benefits they expected for a son who died in a war."

"You said it was 'non-combat.' What did happen?"

"The day after word came down that his show was canceled and he was going back to simply reading copy prepared by the rest of us, he slipped off base to eat in a little village with this family he'd gotten to know. They offered him *ô mai*—apricot covered by ginger, sugar, and licorice root slivers. He had some kind of allergic reaction—I guess, anaphylactic—to either the fruit or the spices and was dead before morning."

"His heart?"

"No, his throat swelled up. He actually suffocated."

"And no one noticed? No one did anything?"

"The family had gone to bed while he was sitting out front having a cigarette—or a joint, I guess. Mama-san and Papa-san worked on the base and tilled their small garden and made their own clothes and sold hand-made goods in a local market, so they were exhausted at the end of the day."

142

"And the Army? Didn't they notice one of there soldiers was missing?"

"We didn't have roll calls at night or reveille. As clerks and administrative personnel, many with college degrees, they let us pretty much police ourselves. And we knew Johnny often stayed out past curfew."

"So Short-timer Sam was shorter than he realized," observed Cathy sadly.

Jeff folded a dessert menu and then said, "You know, his shortness was real. I'm not so sure ours was."

"What do you mean?" asked Mark. "Though now that you say it, I think I may understand."

"When you and I got short—even though at different bases—we saw our whole time in the Army as near an end." He turned to Cathy and Ann. "If you had less than six months left in your enlistment when you came back from Nam, they let you go."

Mark added. "Of course, you still had four years of commitment to the Army reserves, but no one like us was ever called up, so far as I know."

"So, our Army careers were officially over when we finished out-processing. We went from Short to Out, and yet ..."

"And yet we found in some ways were still 'in.' We got out of the military, but the military never got out of us."

"Right. Only recently have we figured out how different we are from those who didn't serve. And as the percentage of the population at large who volunteer for service gets smaller and smaller ...what is it? one percent?"

"That's what I've read."

"Well, we find ourselves belonging in the multi-generational community of veterans and active duty military, not so much a selective group but one with clear criteria. And our membership in that group will last as long as we do."

"So, we were never really Short-timers. We just thought we were."

Ann gave a strained smile to Cathy. "I think that might have been something Short-timer Sam might have warned the two of you about."

"If he'd told us," said Mark, "I'm pretty sure we wouldn't have heard him."

# Into the Wind

I.

"The roller furling is stuck," Ray yelled, gesturing toward the bow. "We need to secure the jib."

Mark knew the forward sail was called a "jib," but he had no idea what a roller furling was. (It's a mechanism that allows the forward sail to be spooled up on the forestay, thus no longer filling with air).

Ray was coming back from the bow — where'd he'd gone for a diagnosis of the problem — to the cockpit. The wind was howling and the boat was pitching in white-tops; so the older man crouched as he moved in order to stay close to the deck. He also kept a firm grip on the rope railing. This was Mark's first time as a passenger/crewman on the classic 22-foot Herreshoff sailboat, and he was already well on his way to panic.

Ray had the Eagle hauled out of the water over the winter so the bottom could be cleaned and repainted; at the same time he was having hip replacement surgery. So two bodies were being renewed, but the human was 89 years old, the boat a mere 40. Today's outing was a trial run for both.

When Ray invited him on the maiden voyage of the restored boat, Mark at first envisioned a leisurely cruise down the broad river, anchoring for a lunch of bologna sandwiches and cold beer pulled from the cooler in the galley, tall tales told as a soft breeze crossed the cockpit.

Then he thought of Ulysses near the end of his long life. According to the British poet Tennyson, the great Greek warrior resisted retirement, thinking "How dull it is to pause, to make an end, / To rust unburnished, not to shine in use!" Full of such romantic notions, Mark saw himself signing on for adventure, one of Ulysses aged "mariners, / Souls that have toiled, and wrought, and thought with" their leader for decades.

Now he found himself shouting, "Just tell me what to do," his words battling the sharp slapping of the jib, loose at the base, and the splash of waves on the bow.

"Keep her into the wind," Ray called back, pointing toward the big highway bridge crossing the river about a quarter of mile to the east. A strong northeastern breeze was blowing directly through it. The boat would be steady if the bow pointed directly into the wind, which would flow around the sails rather than fill them.

At the time Mark couldn't understand how his senior captain was staying calm. However, two years later at a block oyster boil, when Ray talked about getting his troops on a ship sailing off to war in 1942, he began to understand. That tense encounter—and much that came after it—had been perilous; this, by comparison, was routine.

146

Mark was grateful that Ray at least identified a mark to sail toward. He was so new to the seafaring business that, when he was out on the moving water, he couldn't be sure which direction the wind was blowing. Now he lined up the target in his sights and committed himself to keeping it directly over the bowsprit.

Careful to maintain a hold on the boom as he moved, Ray lowered himself into the cockpit and scooped up several bungee cords from the seat. By the time Mark realized he was about to climb back up on the deck, gather the flapping sail in his arms, and wrap the cords around it, the octogenarian was already releasing his grip on the mainsail halyard and stepping forward. The boat was still pitching with the waves, and, for a moment, he would be holding onto nothing.

"Ray," Mark screamed. "Ray, let me do that."

Mark had risen from a sitting position to stand and reached out with his hand, as if his friend would immediately give him the ties and trade places. He should have known that that wasn't going to happen. And if he didn't do his job—keep the boat steady into the wind—Ray would be thrown in the river.

"If he goes overboard," Mark thought, "I might as well as well jump in after him …with the anchor roped to my neck." Ray's daughter, Lin, a friend to Mark and his wife Rachel for forty years, would kill him if he let her father fall overboard.

II.

Lin was one of Rachel's best friends from college and had been in the hospital when his daughter came into the world twenty-one days earlier than expected. Hearing an uncertain heartbeat during labor, the doctor explained that a Caesarian delivery was necessary. Lin, a pediatrics nurse, stayed with Mark through the night.

Responsibility for the infant's first checkup two weeks later fell to Mark. In those days new mothers could not ride in cars so soon after an operation for fear the stitches would be jarred loose. But Lin volunteered to ride to the doctor's with Mark.

"I'll hold her," she told the nervous father, lifting Marian comfortably from Rachel's arms. "And you just be the reliable, steady driver." Mark, nervous about every procedure in infant care, accepted this proposal immediately and marveled at how calm Marian was in Lin's arms. Rachel smiled a wan thank-you and reluctantly waved them on. Another friend was keeping her company for the next hour.

At the hospital Mark felt he was riding on a magic carpet of Lin's reputation. The seas of patients, staff, and visitors parted to let them through the reception station, the pediatric waiting area, the examination room. "You sit here," Lin commanded with Marian completely still and cooing in her arms.

The doctor came through the swinging doors. "Hello, Lin. And what do we have here?"

Should he have taken Marian at that point and

explained that he was the father, that the nurse was the mother's helpful friend? Perhaps. But these were the years when new fathers were essentially bystanders during labor, at the nursery, in the hospital room.

Later, he would regret that he had not been more assertive, the man in charge. But then he also came to understand why he hadn't been: he'd been back from Vietnam for less than a week, and his mind was stuck in New Jersey, the unexpected way station on his return from war.

Eventually, he concluded that it had been wise to rely on the strength Lin seemed to have inherited from her parents and felt there was no weakness on his part in letting her take charge. Lin became Marian's godmother and later married one of Rachel's colleagues in the biology department graduate program. The two couples remained close.

III.

Miraculously, Mark was able to keep the Eagle into the wind as Ray secured the flapping jib. Then the 89-year-old great grandfather crawled back to the cockpit; but he didn't take the tiller from his nervous assistant. "Keep her steady," he commanded.

"Steady!" thought Mark, "in this wind, with these waves? With my inexperience?"

In fact, though, the boat, now more in the shelter of a cove, was rocking less. And with the jib tight, Mark could pilot more easily.

"Let's get this sail down," announced Ray matter-of-factly, looking up at the large mainsail, gaff-rigged and trapezoidal in shape.

Mark wanted to say "Aye-aye!" as if he understood what was to happen; but he had no idea what to do, or what not to do. It turned out his assignment had not changed.

"Keep her into the wind," Ray repeated as he passed through the cockpit and sat down by the motor. Switching the fuel cock to open, pumping the choke knob a couple of times, he yanked the starter cord and the engine caught.

"Thank goodness," thought Mark. "Now he'll motor us in." They were only about half a mile from shore, where Ray kept the Eagle moored to a buoy fifty yards out.

But, rather than bring the boat about, Ray kept the engine at a low idle, passed Mark again in the cockpit, and went forward to unhook the halyards and begin lowering the gaff. Mark tried to help bunch the sail on the top of the boom as it came down, but realized he was letting the boat slide off course.

"Give me some of those ties," Ray said, gesturing into the cabin, where there was a pile of canvas straps. Mark hesitated, not wanting to let go of the tiller. But then he didn't want his skipper to go after them himself; so, as quickly as he could, he leaned in, snatched a handful, extended them to

150

Ray, and grabbed the tiller again.

"Into the wind," he thought, looking to the bridge, his mark. He tried not to assess the darkening clouds above it, the gusts of wind still pulling at the mainsail. If he somehow got safely back to port, he'd never go out on the Eagle again.

Of course, they did get in, and he went out with Ray on many occasions over the next few years, often packing lunch so they could use the whole day. His voyages took him down the river of time to his friend's WWII past and to his own time in Vietnam.

IV.

Mark and Rachel had come to Hartford, a village in northeastern North Carolina, with the intention of retiring from their past: two academic careers in central Virginia. Restoring the two-story frame house on the water would be just the passtime to draw them away from the emotional roller coaster of watching higher education evolve from an academic enterprise into a corporate business.

They had been in Hartford a number of times when Lin was visiting her parents. The two couples—Mark and Rachel, Lin and Ross—had remained friends since graduate school; and Hartford was a convenient meeting place. The children—two to each family—knew each other from many shared vacations. So it seemed a kind of destiny when Lin said that summer, "you have *got* to see this house!"

151

Her aunt had been the last to live in the old family home, keeping an adult son beyond the time she was able to manage it and him. A hoarder who saw no one but his mother, Lin's middle-aged cousin had filled five bedrooms with uneven stacks of magazines and newspapers, electrical appliances (some in their original packaging), canned and dry goods in irregular piles. The tour followed a path that seemed to be a combination of steeple chase and miniature golf course.

When the elderly mother and her son died, within six months of each other, Lin's parents were satisfied to sell the home to their daughter's good friend, someone they already knew. And Mark began to pursue a prairie native's fantasy: sailing.

After the scary first trip out, he logged many satisfying cruises. And the captain gave helpful lectures about sailing, at one point explaining the value of the jib.

"You can see that it's smaller than the mainsail and triangular in shape, but the big sail functions more efficiently at a higher angle of attack with the jib out front."

"Ah." Of course, Mark didn't understand this any more than he understood the difference between the true wind (what a stationary person feels) and the apparent wind (what someone on a moving boat feels).

"When it's set correctly, there's less chance of flow separation and stalling. Keeps a steady course."

152

"Ah."

Mark concluded only that two sails were better than one. He also came to realize that the twinges of anxiety he felt during voyages almost always came from such ignorance of basic seafaring lore.

"Take the tiller, Mark," Ray instructed him on one outing. The captain had steered them through the bridge channel; and now the seven-mile stretch of open river down to the Albermarle Sound spread out before them.

"All right. But give me a point to aim for."

"Middle of the river, south south-east. Wake me if anything comes up."

Wake him? Mark couldn't believe he was to be left in charge!

At least Ray didn't go below, where there were cushioned bunks. He ate the last of his Oreos, took a swig of coffee, and stretched out on the bench opposite the one Mark was on, tilted his hat over his eyes, and—as near as his amateur first mate could tell—fell asleep immediately.

Mark nervously studied the clouds, wondering about how the sails were set. Did he hear thunder in the distance? What if other boats came close? Who had the right of way? Should one approaching traffic on the starboard or the port side? Hell, which *was* the starboard and the port side?

He learned, of course, that Ray knew the river

153

as well as he knew his wife of sixty-four years—Penny's moods, the changes, weather around them. The soft north wind would carry the Eagle so gently that Mark could have let the rudder have its way for an hour. If it had not been so, Ray, Ulysses come again, would not have taken his nap.

V.

During Ray's dozing, Mark recalled one assignment that had taken him onto water in South Vietnam—well, barely on water. His CO wanted one of the radio specialists to record the sounds of a riverine patrol near Tay Ninh, and his number came up, despite the fact that he was the unit's official short-timer.

"Hey, one daylight cruise in a tropical climate, what can happen?" joked Bernie back at the office. "Besides, if Charlie is watching, he'll think your tape recorder is a Claymore and leapfrog his buddies into the bush."

Army radio correspondents carried cassette recorders about the size of a cigar box (or the portable anti-personnel mine). Major Antinous had become obsessed with producing authentic sounds of war for use in military documentaries. His outfit did not have television equipment, but the photographers and radio specialists could produce effective slide shows with sound tracks. He sent men out to hang onto APCs (Armored Personnel Carrier), to eavesdrop on night ambushes, to ride in helicopters.

"How about you take my spot?" Mark said to
154

Bernie. "You know how to handle the tape recorder and a camera—two for the price of one. I'll take care of production for you when you get back. You, know, the hard part—actually writing a script."

"Sorry," his colleague argued. "Still struggling with that TB hospital story. Can't seem to get the right lead ..."

Bernie was officially assigned to do radio but had more civilian experience as a print photojournalist. He was notorious for self-proclaimed "writer's block." Like others in the office, of course, he was taking his time with unnecessary research and bogus technical difficulties to avoid being sent out again.

The Major wanted the sounds of water lapping on a dock, propellers churning through water, anchors being cranked up from the bottom. Mark was fine with all that. But he hoped not to be recording the sharp commands of action, rounds pinging onto the hull of a PBR ("Patrol Boat, River"), return fire from the .50 caliber machine guns and 20 mm cannon.

He wasn't even happy riding in a Jeep out of Tay Ninh City to a swampy river bank. They called what he traveled a road, but the two tire ruts winding through jungle were more a wilderness trail to him. Assured the area was secure—dawn to dusk, at least—he tried not to look left or right for the twenty-minute ride. The jeep, driven by another correspondent, veered and bumped so much that, when Mark arrived, he felt like a botched James Bond martini—shaken and stirred.

"Holy shit," Petty Officer Eumaeus responded when Mark explained his assignment. "I'm not taking you out. We'll record all this right here."

Looking at the boat, docked for repairs, Mark understood: there was a gaping hole at the water line that had been plugged with a life-jacket by a fast-thinking gunner's mate; he saw too many bullet holes to count; one of the two diesel engines was no longer connected to its water jet propulsion pumps; and a seaman was working with conspicuous bandages on both arms.

The crew of four got into the act, though, splashing water over the deck, banging tools on metal surfaces, racing the single functional engine. The seaman told Mark to put his microphone down low in the cockpit, and the rest shouted orders and responses, rolled supply barrels on the deck, even fired off a few quick bursts from a machine gun.

Mark play-acted earning his sea legs, leaning this way and that and holding onto the railing as if they were pitching into waves. When they were done, Eumaeus said, "Now, you cut and splice, edit and amplify, give the Major what he wants. Any questions, send him to me. I'll find a place for him on our next mission—headed into the shit."

VI.

Being on the water in Tidewater North Carolina presented no dangers equivalent to that day beside the water of the Vam Co Dong River.

Even the day Ray and Mark had to reef the mainsail because of high wind presented no challenge the steady Hartford native hadn't faced before and wasn't ready to deal with again. That day the crew realized they needed to pee, though, required ingenuity and extra balance.

As Mark was straining to keep the tiller he held from dragging him off the bench, Ray observed, "The Eagle came equipped with a wheel, you know, not a tiller." Today the mast was slanted at a 45-degree angle in the strong wind, with gusts occasionally pulling the boat to the point that water raced over the gunwale. Both men had their feet braced against the opposite bench, their bodies vertical and the deck nearly so.

Mark grunted as he spoke. "Would that …make the boat …easier to steer?"

"Harder, but the pull wouldn't be so great as it is with a tiller." He gestured. "Of course, the oversized jib I have adds to the strain. You could probably use a bit of help there to keep her steady."

Yeah! Mark thought. Both of his arms were tiring, and he worried they might start shaking. He assumed Ray would either add his strength or take over completely. But the senior took a half-inch line attached to a cleat on the rail, looped it around the tiller, and told Mark to hold the end. "Easier?" he asked.

"Much." The line took the strain, but Mark still had to make sure his grip was secure. And the bit of relaxation that came with the easing of tension in

157

his arms made him aware of his bladder. An extra cup of coffee before setting sail had clearly been another of his novice mistakes. Even if there were something to use below, he was too embarrassed to ask.

"Can you hold it?" Ray asked, and at first Mark thought he was referring to his pee. But Ray was gesturing at the line. "Got to visit Johnny." He nodded into the cabin.

"Johnny?" thought Mark.

In a minute Ray held up a long-necked, gourd-shaped flask. Mark didn't understand, until the captain turned his back to him, braced his feet against the two sides of the frame that held the door going into the cabin, and began fumbling with his pants.

"When I was a boy," Ray called over his shoulder, "we just went over the side. But now, reputable folks are out on their riding mowers or lifting mint juleps on their shaded docks." He waved at the north shore, where there were fine single-family homes on large, grassy lots. "So, have to observe decorum." Mark realized Johnny was a portable urinal.

"You need it?" Ray asked, after he was done. "I had to have it special made, you know. The one that came with the boat was too small."

Mark wasn't anticipating locker-room humor from an octogenarian, but he caught on after a second. "Right! I ...uh, *think* it's large enough for me."

Ray winked. "I always felt bad for the previous owner …and his equipment." Then he knelt on the bench, emptied and rinsed Johnny over the side. Fortunately the wind had died down a bit, so he was not in danger of falling overboard. Then it was Mark's turn.

"I'll tell you when I thought I'd wet my pants," Ray said to Mark's back as the younger man braced his feet in the cabin doorway and tried to unzip his fly.

"Yeah?"

"Getting a company of black recruits onto a troop carrier in New York City. We were headed to Europe, and they didn't want to go."

Mark understood: most of them draftees, they were being taken into harm's way to preserve their second-class citizenship in America. He suspected Ray, an officer, was armed, the troops not. A volatile situation he knew from fraggings in Vietnam.

"Mutiny?" He guessed that Ray had been put in charge because he had grown up with blacks in this rural community.

"Damn near. Of course, I didn't want to admit that I was scared, too, headed overseas. I'd left a girl back home, so I worried about what we'd get into. And if we'd get out of it!"

He paused as Mark turned around, Johnny in

hand. Then he added, "Penny and I waited five years to get married. She had a hard time of it back home while I was gone — teaching school on a tiny salary, had to stay in a boarding house, the war news ..."

Mark had heard Lin's mother talk about waiting for letters from the other side of the world — three and a half years!

"I tell you what saved us all," Ray went on. "Two black NCO's took command where the white officers could not. Those guys kept order without ever pulling out a weapon. From what I understood, though, some fisticuffs did occur."

Mark wondered if those men were considered heroes or traitors by their communities back home. "The unit stayed together?"

"Three years building roads and airfields across India and Burma. Yeah, we learned to take care of each other. But the world has never been the same since we got home."

Mark understood this as an understatement. The post-war period appeared benign at first, but then the upheavals of Civil Rights, Women's Liberation, the anti-war movement put the country on a rocky course that, Mark felt, had never smoothed out.

VII.

Three and a half years in the Army, no furloughs, no R & R's — the duration. That's what Ray's generation had faced in World War II. And

160

their travels to other continents under difficult conditions had closely followed the Depression, which had seemed interminable also.

Mark, on the other hand, was in the Army for twenty-two months, in Vietnam only nine. He'd gone over with eleven months left in his two-year hitch, then got a six-week drop as part of Nixon's commitment to reduce troop strength leading up to the 1972 election. Warren Stevens got killed, Mark was assigned to be an escort, and another fourteen days of his tour were eliminated so he could be on the same Freedom Bird as his friend.

While he was with the Stevens family for the military funeral, Rachel went into labor at thirty-three weeks. Mark got back to Atlanta six days after she had delivered Marian. He'd been 72 hours in New Jersey helping to fold a flag. He looked forward to ...well, to the rest of his life in a world of peace.

In retirement now, he realized he might finally learn the advantages of a jib, the knots any sailor should be able to tie, how to fall off in a stiff breeze. But he felt he'd never achieve the self-command of his neighbor Ray, his wife, and their contemporaries. Even Lin, with all her magic, would be a notch below her parents. Still, it might not be too late to profit from association with his stoic tutor, who like Tennyson's aged Ulysses, after decades of war, travel, and rule, insisted: "Though much is taken, much abides; and though / We are not now that strength which in old days / Moved earth and heaven; that which we are, we are ..."

161

# Hadrian's Wall

I.

"You're two out of three, now," Grant said as they boarded the bus leaving Stonehenge.

"Well, you *did* promise," replied Cleo. "Now take me to Hadrian's Wall."

When he'd proposed she and the children come with him for his month-long research trip to England, Cleo had said yes *if* she could visit Downs (Charles Darwin's home), Stonehenge, and Hadrian's Wall.

"I can see why you'd like the first two, but why Hadrian's Wall?"

Cleo taught biology, so touring the home of the man whose work separated myth from science concerning human origin was an obvious choice. She would even follow Darwin's "sandwalk," the path he built through the grounds so that he could exercise and think without interruption.

"I'm not sure exactly," Cleo answered. "I read a story in *National Geographic* about it, and it just seemed interesting."

Grant had no trouble understanding why she wanted to tour Stonehenge either, the ancient calendar made of stone. He wanted to see it as an historic artifact, too, but also as the site of one of his favorite novels, *Tess of the D'Urbervilles*. In fact, part of his reading this summer would be in *The Graphic*, the magazine that serialized a version of Thomas Hardy's classic before it appeared in book form.

Cleo explained, "The Romans came that far north, you know, then build Hadrian's Wall. Depending on which side you listen to, they decided that would be the farthermost border of their empire or the wild tribesmen of the region blocked their advance."

Grant didn't have much desire to seek out such monuments of past conflicts, maybe because memories of his experiences in Vietnam were recurring more frequently as he approached middle age. "I don't know," he said, "now that the Berlin Wall is gone, I'd rather celebrate the places where people have connected rather than divided. But," he added giving her a kiss on the cheek, "if you want to see Hadrian's Wall, I'll get you there."

At the end of the trip, he would claim he had succeeded, but it was possible he had let himself be fooled. In his most honest moments, Grant even wondered if he had deliberately taken a wrong path in order to avoid confrontation with the world's past ...and his own. Perhaps what he did on that excursion had something to do with what happened to his friend, Lawrence Price, in a boat on the South China Sea.

II.

Cleo had been the guide for the family

excursions in England, reading the brochures, studying maps, collecting train schedules. Grant had to spend time each weekday at the British Museum researching nineteenth-century periodicals, trying to define the line that separated middle-class writing from high culture literature. (He was beginning to think there was no such division.) Cleo, Marian, and Jack used those hours to take in museums (the Tate), shop for mementoes (Harad's), and see the sights (London Bridge).

The three weekends of their stay were devoted to Cleo's conditions for travel, though she connected the last to two days in Scotland. Her plan was to take a fast train to Newcastle, local trains to and from the Wall, and another express on to Edinburgh. The plan was perfect, the execution less so.

"Have you explained where we're going today?" Grant asked once they were settled on the train. They had seats facing each other with a table between. He planned to teach the kids how to play chess while Cleo studied the guidebook.

"Many years ago, hundreds really," she began, setting her book down on the table. "The Roman empire spread across most of Europe, the Middle East, even parts of Africa." Marian was thirteen, so this made sense to her. At ten, Jack understood the basic geography, but history generally didn't register.

Grant added, "The known world."

"The Pax Romana—peace of Rome—spread
164

through England, or at least the southern part of the island. But north of a certain point, the people, fierce war-like tribes, wouldn't yield to foreign rule. And the Emperor decided it wasn't worth the cost of subduing them. So, he built a wall across the country to protect his towns and cities, keeping the 'barbarians' on the other side."

"Like the Great Wall of China," noted Marian.

"Exactly."

Jack asked, "The Wall's still there?"

"Parts of it are, and it's nearly 2,000 years old. So we're going to see the ruins. And we'll learn about history."

"Right now," said Grant, "let me tell you about the King and Queen, the white and black pawns, knights, and castles."

And as they played, or learned to play, Cleo reviewed the maps. They would change trains in Newcastle-on-Tyne, take about 45 minutes to get up to Hexam, ride a bus out to the site, and have over an hour to look around. They would be in the area before noon, plenty of time to get back for a fast train, which departed at 4:00. They'd made reservations at a B & B in Edinburgh. It stayed light until 10:00 this time of the summer, so they'd be settled in well before it was dark.

What she didn't count on was friendly advice from a fellow passenger, presumably a local, on the train from Newcastle. That exchange altered their itinerary.

III.

Grant had played a lot of chess on his tour in Southeast Asia. He'd tried to teach Larry Price the simpler game of checkers, but his friend couldn't remember all the rules and kept blundering into traps. Larry's denseness was legendary, but his good nature protected him from direct affront. It did not protect him from shrapnel.

Grant remembered the dare his fellow Coastie, Jenson, liked to make: "Light a cigarette on deck," he would say to any newbie. "We're too far from shore for the NVA to pick you off. And it drives them crazy to see us out here."

"I don't smoke," Larry said to Jenson. He was the only man who didn't. But Grant knew that, if he did, Seaman Price, the most trusting soul he'd ever met, would light up right then.

These men were among the few Coast Guard units deployed to Southeast Asia, providing security in ports and patrolling shallow waters like the Cua Viet River, less than a mile from the DMZ. Ninety-nine percent of their duty was routine, if not boring.

Their 82-foot boat occasionally drew enemy fire from the shore; the North wanted to protect their infiltration routes into the South. They were outgunned, of course, as Navy artillery from bigger ships would be called in for support, as well as Air Force fighters. So far in their one-year deployment, no one in Grant's outfit had received a scratch.

None of these men had foreseen duty overseas, despite the fact that their enlistment papers stipulated that it was always a possibility. When they'd signed up, it seemed a great way to avoid Vietnam. After what happened, they wondered if they might have been safer volunteering for the Marines.

IV.

"You can get out at Hexam, sure," the middle-aged woman on the train to Carlisle told the Perry family. "But if it's a bit of an adventure you'd be wanting — off the beaten path, you know — take the Bardon's Mill stop. A nice walk through the fields, that is. And you won't be surrounded by tourists."

"How long will it take?" Cleo asked. "We're on a tight schedule."

"Less than an hour from the station. My advice? See the countryside."

So, wanting to avoid being taken for typical Americans abroad — using their money to ride with fellow countrymen in air-conditioned comfort to all the famous places — they decided to hike the path out of Bardon's Mill. According to their fellow traveler, it would actually save time overall, as the buses from the railroad station to the museums, she claimed, were not always on schedule.

Over the years they came to feel they'd made the right decision, if for the wrong reasons, because they learned more than the facts of history on this expedition. But at the time, hiking through woods, across sheep fields, and over rocky hills, they began to feel that they'd been duped.

"That lady is telling her friends at the pub right now how gullible Americans are," Cleo complained, as she demonstrated to the children how to use the stile to get over the fence. "We might as well be snipe hunting."

"Courage, my sweet. I promised you'd see Hadrian's Wall, and I'm sure we're getting close." He'd estimated they could walk a mile in less than half an hour. So the hike shouldn't take more than 45 minutes. They liked to camp in the Ozarks near Lake Wappapello, and the children were used to day-long hikes in moderate terrain.

"I don't know. Remember what the old guy in the village said." Coming from the tiny railway station, they'd passed a man in overalls working in his garden. Cleo asked him where they could find the path to Hadrian's Wall.

He leaned on his hoe and nodded north. "Th' say it's down off Station Road, quarter mile or so. I b'lieve there's a sign off the road."

"Oh. And how long is the path? We want to hike out, take a look, come back for the afternoon train down to Edinburgh.

"Well, can't rightly say about that. Lived here all my life, but never been to see that wall." He winked and turned back to his row of cabbages. "I presume it'll be there if I ever take an interest."

As they continued on Station Road, Grant

explained, "It's just like us. We've lived most of our lives in Cape Girardeau, but until people came to visit, we never thought about going to see the old Jefferson School."

"Right," Cleo huffed. "That was all your cousins from Boston, thinking they were crossing the Mason-Dixon line and entering the dangerous world of the Deep South. If our neighbors had learned they were Northerners, they feared they'd be run out of town."

She and Grant had been offended by the superior attitude of their visitors from the North — as if Boston didn't have its race problems!

While public schools were segregated in Cape until 1954, the community complied with the Supreme Court Decision. The original school for blacks, John S. Cobb School, burned in 1953, so the most visible sign of the past was gone. But Jefferson School was still standing.

With Cobb School gone, white students had been moved out of Jefferson to Mary Greene, and blacks attended Jefferson until 1955. Then integration removed the barriers. The Jefferson School eventually became an apartment building, though a historical marker had been erected at the site. One of the visiting cousins called it an "apartheid" building.

"Are you sure we're on the right path?" Marian asked, looking ahead. They were crossing a pasture bordered by woods. And, while the ground was worn, suggesting a trail, they had seen no markers

169

since they left Station Road. There they had read it was roughly two kilometers to a point where you could see the Wall.

"We've come about the right distance, I think," said Grant, checking his watch. "Let's get up on the top of the next rise, where we'll have a view of what lies ahead."

Marian reminded him, "They're called 'downs,' Dad." Earlier Cleo had interrupted their chess lesson to explain this reversal of American usage.

From the 'down' they looked into a broad valley and saw a road snaking out to a building of some sort with a substantial parking lot. Grant concluded that it was the museum you could reach from Hexam, and the cars and vans in the lot had brought in the tourists. So, the wall had to be right there. And they could see "there."

"Still, let's go for ten minutes more," he suggested. "Maybe we'll come on another section of the ruins."

At the bottom of the down they stepped out of woods and surveyed the next rise. Several hundred yards ahead and above them were large rocks jutting up against the sky. Were they looking at remnants of Hadrian's Wall? Cleo seemed eager to accept what she saw as turrets, milecastles, or wing walls, parts of the ancient structure. Grant worried that she was trying not to sound disappointed, so he argued that they were standing on one side of a glacis and looking over to a berm parallel to the Wall.

170

Whatever was there, they knew they were running out of time and decided to retrace their steps to Barton's Mill, if not at the pace of a forced march, at least at a sustained speed. Back home they would come to tell others they had definitely seen Hadrian's Wall, either up close where they stood at the edge of the wood or by the museum from afar on the down.

V.

"Where is the DMZ?" Larry Price asked near the end of his tour. He was staring at the shoreline as if there would be some sort of marker—a flag, perhaps, or even a larger red line like the one you could see on a map of the two Vietnams.

"It follows the 17th Parallel. Don't you see it?" explained Jenson, pointing.

Larry trusted everyone, followed orders literally, believed each person he met would be his best friend. Grant found this oddly refreshing and liked to listen to Larry's tales of life back on the West Virginia farm where he'd grown up.

"What's the 17th Parallel? I don't see that either."

Grant tried to help. "That's an imaginary marker, Larry, like the Equator. The Equator runs around the circumference of the earth dividing the Northern Hemisphere from the Southern. And the DMZ is a ten-kilometer wide strip across the country."

Larry squinted, one eye closed. "Something

that wide, you ought to be able to spot it. I can't see it."

Jenson asked, "You remember sixth grade social studies, don't you Larry? We all made a relief map of the world, with the Equator running straight across. You did pass sixth grade, didn't you?"

Everyone wondered how Larry had passed the entrance examinations for the Coast Guard, especially at a time when there was considerable competition for enlistment. The CO let slip once that Price had an uncle in the Missouri legislature, who may have been able to pull strings. Grant, whose family had no political pull, took that as an unpleasant reminder that America remained divided into privileged and underprivileged classes.

Grant pointed. "See where the tree line fades. That's the Ben Hai River. It's right in the middle of the DMZ."

Larry squinted. "I see that. But I don't see any DMZ. There ought to be a sign or something. Everybody's always talking about it, but it seems to me it's something somebody just made up and we pretend it's out there."

Grant, who had finished his Master's in British literature by that time, decided it would be no use giving a lecture on the French Indochina War, the Viet Minh in the north versus the French and their puppet government in the south. The terms of the Geneva Conference ending that conflict barred all

172

military from entering the Demilitarized Zone, presumably insuring a status quo. And America was still trying to preserve the artificial division of Vietnamese people into two nations.

Grant concluded, "Larry don't you worry about it. The CO knows where it is, and he'll tell us what to do about it."

VI.

The Perrys were back in the village with an hour to spare. But the pace of their walk and the afternoon heat had made them thirsty. They stopped outside a pub, and Cleo went in to see if they had any soft drinks or lemonades. Grant, worried that she would be angry he hadn't gotten her closer to the Wall, didn't remind her that in the last century women wouldn't have been allowed where she was going.

She came out after a few minutes, followed by the bartender, who carried four bottles and glasses on a tray. His size, the white apron, the hearty cheer were what they might have expected from a pub owner.

"This man is being so nice," explained Cleo. "Children aren't allowed inside, so he's letting us sit out here on these benches with our drinks."

"That's very hospitable," said Grant. "Thank you. We've been on a hot hike through the woods."

"I understand, out to see the Wall. That's about all that brings folks to our place these days. But most go on to Hexam, take the tour bus."

173

"Someone on the train said it would be more interesting this way. And the countryside is beautiful."

"We like it here. Most tourists who come through don't pay much attention to our little village, just want to learn about ancient history."

Grant studied him a minute. "Let me make a guess: you've never seen the Wall, have you?"

The big man smiled and shook his head. "Too busy living."

Jack piped up, "They told me it was famous, but all I saw were some big rocks on a hill."

The pub owner chuckled. "Let me explain something to you good folks. Look off the road down about 300 kilometers. See that grey stone building there, with the chickens in the yard, a milk cow on the other side?"

"Sure. Two stories, big doors on the first floor."

"Right. That building is one thousand years old at least. Built with the rock found around here, put together by hand one stone at a time, made to last in a harsh climate. Winter's rough up this way — strong winds, snow, long cold nights. What they'd do in those days is bring the animals in on the ground floor after sunset. Their bodies provided heat for the family upstairs."

Cleo studied the building. "That makes great sense. Saves fuels and protects the livestock from predators. Might be a bit smelly, but you can get

174

used to that."

"That's right. You were also protected yourself from anyone who might want to get in that you didn't want in. The animals would alert you, and you had the upper ground. Those walls are over a foot thick."

"So, not exactly a fort, but a safe house."

"Right again." He gave an approving nod. "Now, if you go ten miles up north—other side of the Wall, you see—you'll find buildings just like this, built way back then, too. The people who live in them are just like us. Why, I've got cousins up by Whiteside who use a building that matches the one you see here."

"Ah," Cleo said thoughtfully. "In other words, your cousins and neighbors are not wild men who paint their faces and go on rampages across the land, as opposed to civilized Romans who wear togas and debate public policy with utmost politeness."

He laughed a third time. Looking at the children's empty bottles, he asked, "More drinks?"

Grant checked the time. "No, thanks. We want to make sure we're on the train. What's the total here?"

"There's no charge, friends. Welcome to Northumberland."

VII.

Lawrence Price was killed by "friendly fire."

The U.S. Air Force saw lights off the coast near the DMZ, couldn't get a radio response, opened up with what they thought were warning shots at an enemy ship. Jenson was offering his cigarette to Larry, holding it out at arm's length, when an exploding fragment went neatly through the other man's eye.

The crew scrambled to stations, frantic radio transmissions went out, the planes returned to their carrier. There was damage to the hull, another Coastie was slightly wounded, a third sprained an ankle racing to his post. There was a long investigation, everyone provided testimony, the matter was closed: a failure of communication, the cost of war.

Grant had been in a long-term chess match with the cartographer. Later he looked at his friend stretched out in sick bay before being bagged. Price's remaining eye was open, as if he were still searching for the DMZ.

# Camp Hoover

Dave Jenson looked down the trail, checked his watch, and made the decision to go. Unless the sign was completely misleading, he'd be back in Harrisonburg in time to meet his wife for the conference reception. The sign read: "Camp Hoover, 1.7 miles."

Sharon was attending a weekend meeting of aquatic biologists at James Madison University. Massive fish kills and human illness potentially related to the parasite, Pfiesteria Piscicida, had brought together government officials, fishing industry representatives, and scientists hoping to explain the dangerous outbreak. She was a key presenter, and he had come along to keep her company at social occasions.

As Dave crossed Skyline Drive from the Milan Gap parking area and entered the woods, he assured himself he would be all right as long as he didn't encounter more than small streams. While he was convinced nothing bad had happened in the jungle outside Tay Ninh, he didn't like to be reminded of that wooded scene along the river.

He didn't actually know what Camp Hoover was, but at least it was a destination. Many trails in Shenandoah National Park simply took you through woods and back to where you had started. That this hike had a goal made it more attractive.

And it was an acceptable length for his one afternoon in the mountains, which, he hoped, might bring him out of the dark mood that had haunted him recently. It did, and then it didn't.

Where the blue-blazed path to Camp Hoover split off from the Appalachian Trail, he amused himself with speculation about his destination. Perhaps, he speculated, Camp Hoover is a retirement home for old vacuum cleaners, machines no longer able to function and put to pasture in a remote shady grove. More scenic than suburban attic or basement, let alone a junkyard, it would be a happy resting ground. Dave could appear to them as an owner from their previous lives.

As Dave got farther from the Appalachian Trial, the sounds of other hikers faded. Judging from the grass under foot and the close branches ahead, he concluded that this trail was lightly used. It might be that he would have the path to Camp Hoover all to himself. A good time for reflection, he decided. The last few months had been troubling, and he wasn't sure why.

He remembered reading about Hoovervilles in Steinbeck's classic, *Grapes of Wrath*. Out of luck farmers from the Midwest would stop along Route 66 on their journey to a fresh start in California. Looking for work to pay for gas, they built temporary shelters with whatever they could find—tents made from bedding, shacks from packing material, furniture out of rusted buckets. Maybe Camp Hoover was an Appalachian version, preserved by the Department of the Interior to teach the lessons of history.

He came to a stream angling down the mountainside. It had carved a small ravine into the rock, but at this high point, it was so narrow he could step across. Further down, he suspected, it might be much larger, fed by run-off and small springs.

The stones he walked on, though, were wet and his foot slipped off the last one. "Whoa!" he said, catching himself just in time. "I think a walking stick might be a good idea here." Knowing that he couldn't break off a limb in this national park, he kept an eye out for one on the ground that would be serviceable.

He imagined himself falling and breaking an ankle. Could he make it back using a stick as a crutch? Perhaps, but at least he had recorded his name and departure time at the trailhead log book. If he failed to return to Harrisonburg by an appropriate time, Sharon would be able to tell the park rangers the make and license of his car. They would find it at the parking lot, inspect the log, and send rescuers. He hoped she wouldn't identify him as a Vietnam vet who'd been troubled of late. That kind of statement was hard to get off the record.

Where had he read that the slang term "hoover" meant a sex act related to the action of a vacuum cleaner? The world was changing, to be sure; but a camp for that? Surely not. Maybe the fact that Sharon had been so caught up in this

Pfiesteria question over the last few months, and didn't seem to have much time for him, was inspiring weird erotic daydreams!

After a switchback going up and then another coming down, he came across a second creek, only slightly wider than the first. His walking stick proved useful in steadying himself as he balanced on the short, one-log bridge.

He felt he'd been balanced in a precarious situation for some time, trying to decide if he should make the jump from working as a mechanic to teaching shop at the high school. They didn't call it "shop" any more, of course, but "automotive technology." Still, with the addition of computers, it had many of the same goals as the classes he'd taken decades ago.

Dave had gotten into the trade after his three years as an Army motor pool mechanic. Experience in the field had taught him to improvise, and that skill stood out in comparison to the ability of many school-trained technicians. Of course, being in the field had not been any fun; but, once he was home, he learned to repress the negative aspects of his twelve-month tour in Southeast Asia.

"Bears!" he said out loud a few minutes later, hearing rustling in the bushes above him on the hillside. In the park literature he'd read that hikers could encounter black bears along the trail, though most animals avoided human contact. "Still," Dave muttered, "I think I'll view my walking stick as a club just in case."

He knew the piece of dry hemlock he'd found would be no real defense against a mother who felt her cub threatened; but the simple assertion was calming. He recalled pretending a similar authority about the wilderness on earlier occasion: his honeymoon at the Peaks of Otter Lodge one hundred miles south on the Blue Ridge Parkway.

"There are two kinds of mountain trails along this scenic route," he had proclaimed to his bride, whose previous trips into the woods had generally been college field trips with her science courses. After their first night at the lodge they were enjoying buckwheat pancakes with wild blueberry syrup at the Lake View Restaurant. "There are 'up' hikes and 'down' hikes."

"No level ones?" she teased. "Like around the lake."He scowled through the plate glass window across the water, where they had strolled the evening before.

"Well, none worth taking. Even if you follow a ridge sometimes, you need to get up there and come down again. As the road winds across the Blue Ridge, you have the option of climbing to some high point, or descending down into a valley."

"Yes," she agreed. "But what goes down must come up and *visa versa*, no?"

"True. However, the goal of an 'up' hike is spiritual, intellectual, a quest for vision. Different from the 'down' hike."

"Ahh. So, up is where you find the Zen master sitting in a lotus position and answering pilgrims' questions about the meaning of life."

"Hrmpph. True seekers need no guides. They reach the top, the 360-degree vista, survey the world below them—now seen as small and petty and limited. He views the heavens and the earth and ...and all that had been worrying him disappears. Whatever ...from the past that had ..."

She touched his arm. "Dave. You okay?" He must have had the mystic's look, a gaze off into the grand scheme of things. Or it could have been one of those troubling memories from the war taking shape in the clouds. They did that frequently in those years.

"Oh, yeah." He gave himself a shake. "Actually, I was already thinking about the other kind of hike, the 'down.'" Their server brought the check and he calculated a modest tip.

"Okay. What's that like?" She folded her napkin neatly and set it beside her plate.

"That's an inner journey, into the depths of the subconscious, back into earlier experiences you can't remember in your daytime thoughts."

"Your infancy or even before, as Freud thought?"

"Well, I don't know about that. But as you descend into a valley—the trail usually follows a stream gathering speed and volume as it goes— you delve into your deepest, darkest thoughts. You

182

enter the terrain of dreams and fantasies."

"Sounds kind of scary to me!" She had looked at him intently.

"It can be," he admitted. They let the topic rest there. It came up, of course, when he entered counseling ten years later.

Dave came to a third creek (actually the first, Mill Prong, now enlarged by a number of feeder streams). "I must be getting close to Camp Hoover. As I remember, this stream was about a mile from the trail head."

He spoke out loud, not quite sure why, though he knew human voices would alert bears to human presence and that they would generally move in other directions. Perhaps, not having heard the sound of a single human since he had left the AP, he also wanted company. Dave paused and listened, wondering if anyone, animal or human, had heard him.

He had felt more comfortable talking out loud to himself after his sessions with Dr. Morgan. So long as he was alone, his therapist had told him, there was nothing wrong with articulating his concerns in any form.

His anxiety then had seemed to be connected to Sharon's remarkable professional rise: winning a prestigious graduate fellowship, gaining a research appointment at NC State, beginning a solid series of publications. Meanwhile he was still working at a garage and watching others be promoted into management ahead of him.

Later, though, Dr. Morgan thought his anxiety might be linked to his experience in Vietnam. Eventually, the therapist had recommended a hypnotist, who claimed she could bury whatever events were causing his unrest so deep they would never surface again. Now he couldn't remember what parts of his tour had been so troublesome.

This time Dave whispered, "*Deliverance!*" remembering the 1972 film with Burt Reynolds in which four city dwellers are ambushed by hillbillies. Unprepared to confront a degraded human nature, two of the businessmen are brutally abused. "I need a bigger stick!" Dave said, this time to himself.

The trail descended more steeply now along a hillside. A high ridge was to Dave's right, and the ground fell away sharply on his left. He could hear water down below, more than the creeks he had crossed. The different streams must all be gathering toward some common destination.

If Dave became an "automotive technology instructor" at the local high school, he and Sharon would be traveling in the same direction, sharing professional interests. He'd be on a more equal footing with her.

Interestingly, before the recent Pfiesteria outbreak, Sharon had begun to feel frustrated about her career. The little known parasite was not a hot topic in biology, it turned out. She had chosen it as the subject of her doctoral research because so little had been done with the organism. And she was convinced her studies would be groundbreaking.

For a time Dave had teased her for being the stereotypical scientist, working in some obscure field that no one—not her colleagues, her department chair, or research funding agencies—thought deserving of precious resources. Then, with fish suddenly turning up dead in Mid-Atlantic rivers—and the Chesapeake Bay—everyone suddenly wanted her research material. The phone was ringing even at home for her to speak on other campuses, to be interviewed by the media, to visit a site. Could this new success be the cause of Dave's own frustrations?

Ahead he saw the tops of trees unlike the chestnut and red oak that had kept him in the shade all the way. He had expected poplar, perhaps, or birch at lower elevations; but as the view opened up more, he saw hemlock scattered throughout a more open area.

"Hello, Camp Hoover," he said softly, spotting rustic log buildings connected by gravel paths winding through a little valley. There were no signs of activity, however, and no sounds. He concluded, "Looks like an abandoned mountain village more than a busy recreational facility."

As the trail leveled off, it merged with a more finished walkway taking Dave into the camp. He could see that buildings had signs—"Guest Cottage," "Town Hall," "Duty Station"—above the

185

doors; and the areas around the log cabins featured rock gardens, wooden benches, and picnic tables. It was eerie, though, with no human inhabitants. Dave felt like a man from the future visiting a ghost town.

He could still hear the creek he'd been following on his left; but up ahead he saw another, faster moving stream. Following its trajectory, he saw that the two would join to create a small river. His mind surveyed the Virginia map, trying to identify the tributaries that filled the Chesapeake Bay to the east.

Vague images from memory also rose in his mind, something or some things drifting by on the water's surface. He might be thinking of the pictures Sharon had shown him—river fish scarred by Pfiesteria, ugly sores marking the flesh where scales had been. Fish just like that could be farther downstream, part of the outbreak the conference was trying to end. But the images shifted in his head, becoming other bodies moving in muddy water. Larger, maybe bloated, what were they?

Then, he reached a sign that explained where he was: a pre-Camp David presidential retreat. Reaching his destination shook him out of his reverie.

Early in Herbert Hoover's term, Dave read, the president sought out a piece of property where he could escape the heat of Washington's summers. He had three prerequisites: close enough that he, family, and guests could drive from the nation's capital for a weekend; near a place with trout fishing (Dave learned that he was now standing at the beginning of the Rapidan River); and high enough (over 1500 feet above sea level) to be free of mosquitos. The sign also stated that the Hoover family left the camp to the nation after his term in office.

"I see," thought Dave, "Camp David in Maryland must have answered more modern presidents' needs for a private getaway. At one time, though, ministers of state, cabinet officials, business tycoons came here to exchange views over drinks and a meal, perhaps shaping the nation at the same time. Now, this seems to be a park no one comes to but stray hikers like me, wandering off the beaten paths along Skyline Drive."

Dave felt he'd had neither the mountain top epiphany he hoped for nor the sudden insight into his own psyche. All he might end up with was a lesson in history. Well, at least it might provide cocktail conversation material at the conference reception. He imagined himself, balancing crab dip and crackers on a plastic plate, a beer in his other hand, describing the rushing waters of mountain streams.

The professional types at these events were never interested in the breakthroughs of automobile manufacturing, so he often read up on the area they were meeting in order to engage Sharon's colleagues. He was careful not to admit he was a wrench jockey. If she was ever embarrassed by his lack of education in these situations, though,

187

she at least never showed it.

He saw a larger building identified as the "Brown House," a forest version, he guessed, of the urban White House. He could imagine Hoover and top aides meeting inside to deal with the economic crisis of the 1929 stock market crash, Black Friday. Dave thought it was sad to see these facilities so empty. Perhaps, he thought, this abandoned site was a reflection of Hoover's reputation for failing to prevent—or even causing—the Great Depression. It seemed unfair.

Nearby was a crude log bench and a sign stating that in this area President Hoover met with British Prime Minister MacDonald to discuss limiting the growth of international military might after the disastrous First World War. "Disarmament!" thought Dave. "Good idea. Too bad it didn't work. First, WWII, then, Korea, then Vietnam, now Desert Storm. Humankind doesn't seem capable of putting down the club."

He realized that he'd walked through the entire camp and was now standing at a gate with a parking area on the other side. He stepped through and looked back over the ground he'd covered. Another sign explained that he was at the end of a road coming south and west from Washington, D.C., to Camp Hoover.

"Ah," he exclaimed. "I've come to the park through the back door. Regular visitors—unlike present companywould drive up here to the main entrance …if there ever were any visitors, that is."

188

It made him feel like an intruder, having snuck through some sort of security to get inside a protected area.

Gazing across the grounds, he saw the abandoned park as if he were looking at an old post card, a faded black and white photo from the time Camp Hoover received regular visitors. A light strand of smoke trailed from the mess hall chimney, people strolled down paths by the river, two men sat on a bench. Hoover and MacDonald, he fancied, discussing an end to war.

Then, as if this were the opening scene of a movie playing in his head, everything came to life—a couple crossed over a stream on a wooden bridge, the cook came out to ring the chow bell, Hoover was gesturing emphatically. Everything was in black and white, a bit jerky as if it were part of a newsreel shown at the movie theater. Still, it seemed to Dave that the world's clock had been turned back to 1929 and he was now a witness to important events.

He decided he should even do more than watch: he could take action.

"Wait!" called Dave excitedly. In his imagination, he had walked back into the camp and was approaching the two heads of state. "Please," he continued. "Don't stop your discussion, Mr. President and Mr. Prime Minister."

Now a player in the long ago scene, he felt he was going to change history. "Don't worry about the stock market," he told the two men, giving a

189

dismissive wave with one hand. "The economy will recover in time, or you can put a bunch of people to work for the government, doing good things for the country. But ...but you need to focus on disarmament."

They seemed interested, so he went on: "Stop building submarines, bomber aircraft, bigger tanks. You can change the course of human events. Rather than being blamed for the Depression, Mr. President, you'll be revered because ... because you prevented millions of deaths. I can't tell you how bad it will be."

He saw their faces brighten with his encouragement, and he felt he was accomplishing a momentous event—re-charting the modern world. But as his spirit soared, the scene began to get fuzzy. The present blurred with his vision of the past, as leaves fell from the trees into the places the two men had been. Dave's vision of past, present, and future was disappearing.

He looked up over the camp to the mountain, searching for the trail he had followed from Skyline Drive and trying to recover his magical power. Through the trees, though, he felt he recognized another landscape, the Ozark woods in which he and his neighborhood pals had played in their childhood. Illogically, it seemed if he could now hike back the way he had come (maybe he should even walk backwards! or moonwalk!), if he traveled far enough, he could return to that innocence, to a time before he even knew about history.

190

He could start his whole life over, it occurred to him. Knowing the challenges that were to come—the bars to promotion, new electronic systems running automobiles, ways to repair a deuce-and-a-half in a tropical climate—he would be ready this time. He'd do better in school, understand how to please his superiors at work, anticipate what to everyone else would be the unexpected.

It would be unfair, of course, to take advantage of this superhuman insight, but—what the heck!—he deserved a second chance.

And, oh! He would woo Sharon more properly this time. He'd be far less assertive, more respectful, appreciating her gifts. His children would find him at home more often, and he'd be less moody. Ah, surely, untroubled by the curves life had thrown him—because he'd see them all coming this time!—he'd roll with the punches, keep his temper, balance all the forces.

"Sir!," said a voice. "Sir! Are you okay?"

Dave turned around. "What? Okay? …am I …?"

He saw a park ranger walking toward him from a government vehicle, his name, "Partner," stitched on his shirt. "Are you Mr. Jenson?" Partner asked.

"Jenson? Yes, Dave Jenson …how did you know?"

"Your wife called us. Said you were due back

over an hour ago. She was worried."

"Oh, I see." Dave glanced over his shoulder, to the sign on one side of the gate. He scratched his head. "I guess I must have lost track of time."

"That can happen. You get away from the familiar …. And the light can be different up here in the mountains."

"Yes, I see. Besides," Dave waved back at the park, "it was fascinating, Camp Hoover. It made me think, you know, about …how things got to be the way they are."

"That happens to some who come here," Partner admitted, though Dave felt he wasn't being sincere. "But, look, I've got the jeep." He pointed. "Can I give you a ride back to the parking area? It would save you retracing the way you've already been, seeing the same things a second time."

Dave hesitated and then nodded. "I guess that would be helpful. I shouldn't keep Sharon …my wife, waiting. Must live in the present, after all. Let the past stay in the past."

"Good thought, sir. Now, um, you can leave that walking stick here …just lean it up against the fence. And we'll get you where you need to be in no time at all."

# Cookbook

When Alice Marie Cook starting talking, there wasn't much anyone could do but listen. "If you all want to have any kind of social gathering," she might say one Sunday, "you've got to start with my Aunt Ida's potato salad."

This could be at the after-church coffee hour, where we sit six or eight to a table or in a cluster of chairs. Alice Marie would get a head of steam up, often about recipes and cooking and her favorite meals from years ago, and keep on chugging whether her audience had heard her tell these tales several times before or not.

"Of course, Ida wasn't really my aunt. She married Walter, who was the first husband of our cousin, Sara Beth, now deceased. Sara Beth was the oldest by about ten years, so we always thought of her as an aunt. And Walter was ten years older than she was, having gone away as a young man to make his fortune somewhere out west, we never knew exactly where except that it wasn't Texas."

Some newer church members might have looked for an excuse to get up — wanting another cup of coffee, pretending to spill and need a napkin, wondering out loud if they should help put things away; but most were resigned and settled in as the captive audience they realized they'd become. Alice Marie would get to a point eventually. And there was pity for her, though the events that explained her sorrow never appeared directly in her ramblings. Many of us are from her generation or the next, and a lot are veterans; so we can fill in from our own stories what's hidden in her ramblings.

"When he'd been a boy," she'd continued, "back home down by New Madrid, our parents' and their friends called Walter 'Wally' because he was shy, always trying to blend into the background, wallflower like, whenever any of them started one of those kissing games. Usually it was that Southall girl, I always heard, though it could have been Matthew, as he liked to come after the girls until he met Betty Lane and she got him straight quicker than the price of ham falls after someone hears about a case of African Swine Fever. Why Ida married Uncle Walter, though, once Sara Beth was gone (may she rest in peace), we never understood except maybe that his garden was always full of potatoes."

The true old-timers in Olive Branch New Church Retirement Home knew that "potatoes" were code. When she said the word, they were alert for a subtle gesture at what had happened to her twin boys a long time ago.

"That's what you start with, a pound of potatoes, which are best if dug right out of the ground that very day, as happened a lot because Walter did have maybe the best plot in town. Now, he didn't have flowers in it. Ida put out the jonquils and the daffodils — I *do* love daffodils — in the
194

border by the Webbs' next door, who had their own vegetable patch, but that was over at Angie's brother-in-law's two streets down where he had better sun. He did, that is, until those oaks across the street grew so big they started to shade the western edge and he wanted the town to condemn them, but Reverend Edwards, who lived in that house until his children started to come back home, blocked that. (Not one of his kids could make it, must be that PK syndrome, Preacher's Kid, who feels the pressure to be all perfect but doesn't really want to because he—well, or she, as girls have feelings, too, and shouldn't be thought of as less than men today—wants to have some fun and doesn't see why everyone else gets to.) Revered Edwards, he *had* some pull with Mayor Budd. And finally he moved to that old house out on Swamp Stink Road (I never will understand why the town let that name stand; it was just what we used to call it even though we knew it was North Street all along) where there was room for Larissa, Kristin, and Della as well as the little ones, who kept on coming like their mothers were hens laying eggs every other day."

Alice Marie's boys loved potatoes in any form—mashed, fried, baked, as hash browns, cakes, fries; but they loved Aunt Ida's potato salad most of all.

"That hard-boiled egg should be chopped really fine, of course, and one piece of celery, which Walter—or 'Wally,' if you prefer—didn't have in his garden but you could get it from Amos'

195

Country Store right across from the bank. Well, it *was* across from the bank until they felt the competition from the new Piggly Wiggly out on Highway 22 and turned that store right around, making the side door the entrance and turning what had been a loading area into a parking lot; so the store was really not across from the bank anymore but down from the Methodist Church, if you know what I mean. I don't know why they ever gave that pitiful little road the number 22; it was just dirt when we were growing up and you'd spot the Lynch boys and their cousin James, barefoot, carrying their fishing poles over their shoulders to see if the perch were biting at Simpson's Pond just past the edge of town where the train to St. Louis snakes down by the river. I wasn't to take the City of New Orleans until many years later when my uncle was honored so nicely for his service in the Salvation Army and I saw the one-legged man who was still working for the railroad after the accident but drinking, on the sly, moonshine out of old mayonnaise jars."

It was hard to believe Alice Marie had ever been married. She played the role of elderly spinster so well and only a few of us ever knew about Jackson, whose whirlwind romance of the postmaster's daughter was the talk of our town some seventy years ago. After giving her two sons identical to each other and pretty much to him, he ran off with a schoolteacher who, they said, would do things in the bedroom his wife insisted were forbidden by the Bible.

"Take 1/2 cup of mayonnaise—some say you can use Miracle Whip, but don't you ever try that if Samuel's wife Charlotte is there as she'll suck her mouth in like she'd just bit on one of those peppers from South America or some spice never heard of in any Bootheel kitchen even if you put your potato in the very same basket Aunt Ida always used to carry. It was woven by her grandmother in Memphis from reeds or grasses and I don't know what all that made it not only the strongest basket I ever saw—it could hold that potato salad and jars of relish and vinegar or, if you wanted to (and some people did, believe you me!) a small bottle of spirits—but also a genuine example of craftsmanship you wouldn't see today unless you get into some museum somewhere, I don't know where it would be any more. If there were any justice on God's earth it would still be where I last saw it—Aunt Ida's potato salad basket, that is—on the sideboard Bagby, the hired man, carried through the flood in '36 to keep the fine cherry from getting warped or stained the way it happened with the old bed Great-grandma wanted to be buried in, but of course we couldn't ever do that."

Alice Marie raised her two boys without ever saying a word about their absent father, and they became strong, upright young men. Did well in all their classes, attended every vacation church school until they were too old to go, and worked summers out on the Hamilton farm, bringing in hay, tending to chickens, herding the goats. They volunteered the day after Pearl Harbor, determined to serve their country and pay back the Japanese.

"Aunt Ida's potato salad basket went everywhere in addition to our family reunions, especially to church suppers where folks brought their very best dish, to be sure, except maybe the Taylors who lived, as you remember, for the longest time with her sister, the old maid who inherited a fortune from their great uncle. He buried the family silver under the barn and forgot where it was until he had that stroke, slept for six months, woke up, and said 'Dig under the third horse stall!' as loud as you could say it right now if you were young and had all your teeth, which, I'm so sorry to say, so many in my generation no longer do. Unless it's that Quentin who married the beautiful woman from France and had girls, which I've never understood because he himself had brothers, two of whom were named 'Lawrence,' though I believe they called one Larry and the other Lawrence to keep them straight especially at church because, it seemed to me, one of them was coming down the aisle every Sunday and all week long at the Revival down by Craft's Creek. Of course, there wasn't an aisle there but just a path through the grass probably made first by the Johnsons' cow until that time her milk went sour after she ate so many spring onions."

At least one of the brothers could have stayed out of combat, as the government wouldn't put two men from the same family in such danger, especially if the mother was without a husband.

But William and Frederick wanted to stay together, and their mother was that proud, so they shipped off to the Pacific and starting island hopping their way to Tokyo.

"A small onion is best for the potato salad, but you can use half of a large one, which is the way they put them out at the store these days, all full of the things they shoot into them at the processing plant over in Sikeston across the street from that house the men used to go after getting paid on Saturday for bringing in the cotton. We girls knew what went on there but could never say anything about it unless it was on a sleepover at Robin's with the covers pulled over our heads and not even a flashlight to show each other's faces. I'm so glad our town hasn't changed that much in all the days since, with the feed store close to the train station and the two banks catty corner to each other at the heart of town helping those farmers who need cash every season for planting and those teachers — bless their hearts! — who can't afford a mortgage on the tiny little bit they pay them unless they get lucky and marry the principal. However, that turned out not to be lucky for Emily Jane Morgan, as her man with the funny name — 'Chapman' was it? — went crazy that Thursday night after the school board meeting and took his dog, climbed up the water tower, and threatened to jump — the both of them — if everyone didn't leave them alone for two weeks straight until they could get the 'damn' budget figured out (pardon my using such spicy language but that's just what he said)."

Twice a month Alice Marie shipped those boys everything they needed to make potato salad — Aunt Ida's, of course — but without the mayonnaise, which would go bad. She sent packages for eighteen months with only a couple of letters coming back to thank her and to say eating that potato salad was like being home in southeast Missouri. We never knew if they really got them or not.

"The 1/8 teaspoon spicy mustard is best, according to Aunt Ida's daughter Susan, if it has been kept in the root cellar, but she was one who liked dark places herself and ended up managing an underground mushroom factory in some town east of St. Louis that had a German name and therefore I won't remember it; but I do know it was on the Missouri River and that she married a man with the same last name as her own. Her mother would send her to get the mustard while the potatoes were boiling in the large pot with two inches of water over them and waiting to be cooled before they were peeled and the pot washed out so you could use it later, although I'll never forget the time Mrs. Smith (who lived over the fence out back) got chased by a bumble bee that came around the screen door while she was washing her large pot because her younger brother had raced out to beat the stuffing (or so he said) out of Jason Reynolds and left it ajar just enough. Shawn claimed Jason had kissed his girlfriend in a canoe where, he protested, she couldn't get away without drowning, though she thought about it just the same. Anyway, that pot sat on the warm stove while Mrs. Smith was hiding from the bee in the firehouse and was never good for potato salad after that."

The rest of us had our men to worry about in those years, and we all came down to the newspaper office to read the latest, including the lists of dead and wounded from our community. For a time there it seemed like we were losing every battle and all our young soldiers, so we expected to learn the worst each day. Alice Marie was always upbeat, however, seeing victory around the corner and her sons returned as heroes.

"Now I always thought it was a good thing that Mrs. Smith got her a new large pot because it came with a baby in it. She'd ordered it—the pot not the baby—from Sears and the delivery man came when she was at the church setting up for Wednesday night Bible study, where mostly they shared the latest gossip and ate ginger snaps; so he left the package on her doorstep and some poor girl opened the box and deposited into the pot the most beautiful little girl baby, later called Patty (though some of the mean boys called her "Potty," which hurt her until she finally, shopping for a spring dress in Cape Girardeau, found her true love). Of course, that young mother didn't mean for Mrs. Smith to cook Patty, and she didn't—unless you say raising her as her own child was getting her ready to serve to some hungry young man. It was just that the large pot must have seemed to that momma a safe place for right then, it not having rained for over a month that fall and the weather turning a bit cool so we wondered if the corn would come in the way it was supposed to or have all those little stunted ears with tiny kernels used by boys with their peashooters down at the Fallen Heroes Town Park to give you a sting on your backside if you weren't watching. The one her niece married, the Butler boy, was always egging on the little kids to shoot the school guard who had a plenty big target, I can tell you that, and in some ways deserved to be stung."

Even when she got the telegram—both boys killed going ashore the fourth or fifth time out there—she wouldn't believe they were lost. She tucked the papers into that little mahogany desk in her parlor, talked about what they'd do when they were home, kept knitting socks, mittens, and scarfs to mail to the troops.

"Cook your eggs in a small pot at the same time you're mashing the potatoes one at a time in a suitable bowl, but keep your eye on both throughout or you'll find one gone like Jenny Sheeler did when Wally's latest dog made off with her hard boiled eggs and hid them in her bed as if she thought they might hatch and give her a full meal of fried chicken one day soon. Of course, she'd swipe anything, even ran off once with the dish that had the celery, eggs, onion, mayonnaise and mustard mixed together, and we never did find where she hid that. And whether Jenny had salted and peppered to taste before it disappeared, we couldn't be sure, as they wouldn't let that dog sleep in the house because of the aroma that almost cost Lisa her true love, the two of them spooning on the porch swing and her not knowing the dog was under there. The other dogs loved Sage (that was the polite name for him), and you could see him leading a pack around town most any day in the week, usually with a basket or a bowl or tea towel he'd swiped from somewhere in his mouth. You might say he was taking a census of folks and their kitchen equipment or maybe gathering his own ingredients to make potato salad himself, though it never would be as good as Aunt Ida's."

Alice Marie must have been visited by the Army at some point, officers bringing whatever could be recovered of those boys—remains, clothing, dog tags. But no one ever saw visitors, so maybe she went up to St. Louis or down to Memphis to tell the government they had it all wrong, those were some other dead boys, leave her be as she deserved to live her own life as she saw fit. Or perhaps there's a double grave down by the old home place we never knew about, no marker or stone or memorial of any kind, dug in the night by men hired from across the river.

"Aunt Ida would spoon the combined mixture into the bowl with the lid that never did fit right she got at her wedding so she had to put tin foil over it before refrigerating. Later she carried that bowl to our house in her basket from Memphis with some extras nestled around it, coming past the Webbs' garden with the shading oak trees, down Main Street along Amos' store and the Baptist church and the two banks—the one with the mural showing town history in pictures, the other portraits of past mayors, with the exception, of course, of Gordon Vandemore, who had to move to Poplar Bluff after he said he wasn't going to wear a suit to town meetings when it was over 100 degrees."

As the years went on, of course, Alice Marie stopped referring to her boys, and everybody else stopped asking. She got to telling these long, convoluted anecdotes, mostly about cooking and recipes, more details than were necessary or appropriate, and we got to listening patiently. Some believed she told her own story in a kind of code, potatoes the sign that her gift to the nation was recognized if not properly acknowledged.

'Up our street Aunt Ida'd come—I can see her right now in my mind's eye—walking with purpose like a train locomotive and not looking to left or right at any goings on in Fallen Heroes Town Park, by the school (the old Frank school, closed now for forty years but always open in our hearts), and past the house on Rust Street where Patty was 'born' (if you'll allow the expression), saying when she stepped up on our porch: 'If you're going to have a social gathering, see to it that the right people are invited, each of them bringing what they do best, and wearing nice clothes, not too fancy but appropriate to the occasion, and watching their language if the preacher comes. You still start, of course, with potato salad, and I've got mine right here, thank you very much.'"

# Look-alike

When his new son-in-law submitted a photograph of himself to the national Jimi Hendrix look-alike contest, Harold Schure was bothered but didn't know exactly why. Of course, that Andrew was white made the idea odd to begin with. He was also a conventional young man working his way through college on a co-op program with the chamber of commerce. He did not play a musical instrument, and he had been a faithful member of Fairfield Church of Salvation since the age of thirteen. So his pretending to be a rebel rock musician was contradictory in all sorts of ways.

Still, it would take Harold months to realize all the sources of the uneasiness he felt in connection to this event. By then Drew had been declared the winner and was taking Christine to Las Vegas for the celebrity look-alike photo shoot. All expenses were paid by the advertising company that sponsored the contest, and he would come home with a $5,000.00 check.

A unsettling to Harry in the end was his own reliving of an unlucky moment in his past, his best friend's death in South Vietnam. History was, he felt, a world of inexplicable coincidences.

"We could use the money," Harry's daughter had offered by way of explanation to her parents back in October. "We need some things for our

205

apartment — a washer and dryer, for instance. Drew wants to buy the latest X-box, and I've always wanted to see 'Sin City.'"

Harry was puzzled at her desire to travel to Vegas and at her use of the city's nickname. Ever since she'd met Andrew, she had adopted his fundamentalism and frequently talked about the dangers of temptation. Harold felt a double standard somewhere.

His wife, who sometimes complained to Harry that their only child didn't resemble either of them in appearance or temperament, was unsympathetic. "When we got married, we lived in a basement apartment and had to account for every penny we wanted to spend against what we could earn."

Donna had met Harry when he was training to be an Army cook at nearby Fort Leonard Wood. When they married, his corporal's salary plus her grocery store checkout clerk's income barely had them over the poverty line. "No gift from heaven helped us get ahead," she concluded. "In fact, it was your father's combat pay that allowed us to buy our first car."

"Frankly," Harold explained, "I've always been suspicious of windfalls. They inspire unreasonable expectations. It's like winning the lottery. The lucky ticket holders think they're destined to be favored forever, so they spend everything, go into debt, and irritate all the people they don't give money to."

His life had been dramatically changed by the opposite of a godsend: being number 1 in the 1969

206

lottery for the military draft. He had counted on his student deferment keeping him out of the service, but because his birthday fell on September 14, the first date drawn out of the glass jar, it was certain he would be called up and likely end up in Vietnam. How he became a cook was an anomaly: nothing in his education or work experience prepared him for that assignment.

Christine dismissed their concern. "Oh, Drew's not going to win. It's just fun to fantasize. He has to work while he's in school and over the summers. Plus we both study so much that we don't have any time for recreation."

She was an undergraduate sociology major at South Central State University. She and Drew had been able to spend only two nights at Branson after their wedding (last October during their fall break). Knowing friends whose parents paid for trips to Reno or Atlantic City, they felt they'd been cheated.

Both sets of in-laws, however, worried that they were marrying too young (21 and 20) and without sufficient prospects. Prepared to help them for a time with rent and car insurance, they told the couple they would have to finance their own honeymoon. They were also quietly glad the marriage hadn't been made necessary by an accidental pregnancy. But they knew each young person already carried credit card debt (and didn't understand how interest compounded) and had a lot to learn about being on their own.

As the weeks went by, Harry noticed a change

in the way the two viewed their prospects.

"Andrew prayed about it, Daddy," Christine explained one day. "And God answered him. Look at these photos. You can't deny the resemblance."

Harry had to admit it was eerie. Andrew had dressed in bellbottom jeans and a leather vest over a long sleeved T-shirt, teased his hair, and held a borrowed guitar left-handed across his hips. Christine drew a slim fake mustache on his upper lip, and he mastered an angry scowl. Harry could almost hear the blaring feedback, the wah-wah peddle, the distortion behind the black-and-white images.

He remembered the first thing Christine had said about him, that he had a wonderful Avatar on X-box Live. His computer self-image resembled John Travolta in *Saturday Night Fever*, another character far removed from the mild-mannered Midwestern business administration student who aspired to a career in business.

Harry asked—he thought, tongue-in-cheek— "So God's will is going to grace you with a vacation and a cash prize?"

"Stranger things have happened. Remember what the Bible says: "Even the hairs of your head are all numbered. Fear not, therefore; you are of more value than many sparrows.'"

Harry didn't know what to say. Although he attended church—initially so that his children would have religious training—he could never take scripture that literally. An insurance salesman, he calculated the odds—life expectancy, health conditions, family medical history—and used actuary tables to predict outcomes.

When Andrew got the call, he said it was as if he'd been chosen by God. "It was not like any voice I'd ever heard over a telephone," he said in awe. "It was deep, resonant. I'm sure that the Spirit was talking through him."

It's a damn advertising company, thought Harry. Of course they have trained announcers for such events! They're not likely to leave anything to chance.

Christine marveled, "There were thousands and thousands of entries. It can't be simple chance that Drew was selected. It's …it's destiny."

The question of destiny took Harry back to the year he'd spent with Jonah near Da Nang, South Vietnam—well, nearly a year. His friend had said on the day they met, "If there's a bullet out there with my name on it, so be it. Destiny."

They'd come from different stateside bases to join the 1st Engineer Battalion, which supported marines in combat operations throughout the region. A cook and supply clerk, they were on a base, where the chances of survival were much better than in the bush. (Of course, you could still happen to be where a stray rocket or mortar landed.)

Everyone also told them that, coming late to

the war, they'd get home safely. With peace talks ongoing, officers didn't want to risk lives. And both North Vietnamese and Viet Kong units, anticipating the U.S. withdrawal, were avoiding major battles. Still, Harry was suspicious of logic that conveniently predicted a happy return to civilian life in 365 days.

What in the end seemed responsible for Jonah's death, at least to some, was his uncanny physical resemblance to General Creighton Abrams.

"God has a plan for Drew, Daddy. This is just the beginning. He was meant to win this contest so he could do His work in the world."

"Um, do you mean he's going to start a charity to help the poor and the destitute?"

"Nothing like that, Sir," Andrew explained. "Those efforts, no matter how well meaning, always fail. No, the way to help others is to help yourself. I'm going to start a company that will create jobs. And people who want to lift themselves up can come work for me."

"After the semester is over, he's going to take the $5,000 prize money—well, the $3500 we have left—and buy a franchise in VitaLife. They sell dietary supplements and homeopathic medicines that have been shown to work, if the customer believes they will."

"Ah, so it's a matter of faith, like putting hands on someone?"

"Drew has done that! Why, he cured my sprained ankle with one treatment of VitaRub. Now he can reach out to others. We can run the business while still finishing our degrees." She paused. "But, if it goes as the corporation promises, we won't need to."

"And I won't leave you out, sir. You can buy in at the ground level and be guaranteed a good return for many years. The more licensed VitaMen we enroll, the larger our network and the greater the profit. You get a portion of whatever any of your enrollees make in the future. It adds up, I can tell you."

Harry didn't want to hear more. They would be at the bottom of a pyramid that fed the few at the top. Still, he hoped to show his daughter how the cards were stacked against their realizing a return on their investment, let alone the fortune they were anticipating. (Of course, he also knew losing their money would be a happier outcome in the long run than they could guess.) He waited until a week after their return from Nevada and they were preparing for final exams to make his last effort at education.

"I think I understand," he told the couple on their customary Thursday night dinner at Harry and Susan's. (On Sunday night, they had dinner with his parents.) "But let me review what's happened so far to make sure I have the right ideas. I mean, it all starts with Jimi Hendrix, right? If he hadn't become famous, there wouldn't have been a contest, you wouldn't have won, and you wouldn't have the money to buy into VitaLife."

Andrew hesitated, but then admitted, "Yes, though it's possible I might resemble a different celebrity ..."

"Well, okay, agreed." He glanced up as Donna went to check on her made-from-scratch spaghetti sauce, which had been simmering since they got home from church. She would serve it with the roasted winter squash and onion turnovers she'd made several weeks ago and frozen for later use.

Harry went on. "As it is, though, God's plan for you begins with Jimi Hendrix, a rock music sensation whose performance inspired a whole generation. And, of course, he — or his agent or his producer or his record company — made millions of dollars on his talent. And that legacy made the look-alike contest possible. People he made rich put on this event, and you became another benefactor of his fame and fortune, if a small one."

"Daddy, these things happen all the time. People become famous, and their lives affect all sorts of people they never knew."

"Again, I see that." Harry rubbed his chin. "Still, I can't quite think Jimi Hendrix played music just so you would receive a surprise cash gift one day 40 years after this death. Did you know, by the way, that he was in the Army?"

"The Army? I wouldn't have thought that."

"God does work in mysterious ways. From this point in history, it doesn't seem to fit in with his

212

character. But one could say his later success was inspired, at least in part, by his military service. You see, he was given a choice, after getting into some trouble as a youngster: prison or the Army. It was 1961, no war on the horizon—well, none that he could see—so off he went."

Harry decided not to say that it must have been God's will that Hendrix had been unlucky enough to get caught riding in stolen cars, that his destiny included a single unhappy way to stay out of prison, and that his weeks at Fort Campbell, Kentucky, were meant to strengthen his faith.

Returning from the kitchen, Donna chimed in. "In those days all the men were subject to the draft, if they were healthy. The only question was which branch and how long." She smiled at Harry, and he knew she was pleased with herself. Her dishes took a lot of work, but she was proud when these family dinners went well.

"That was true for my generation, sons of the WWII vets; we all expected to go in." He and Donna had talked recently about how few in the next generation, their children, thought about serving in the military. He went on. "You realize what 'universal' conscription means when you see the new recruits like yourself in formation. Their heads are shaved, and they're wearing identical stiff new fatigues. They look amazingly alike."

Andrew said, "I'd like to think some stand out as individuals, not just duplicates of an archetypal GI Joe."

213

"True, some don't fit it. As it turned out," continued Harry, "Jimi was one. He couldn't make it without his music, lost with no guitar. So, after awhile, his father shipped it across the country to him."

"Fathers do take care of their children," smiled Christine as Donna motioned for them to step to the table. Once the dishes had been passed and everyone was settled, Harry returned to his topic.

"It was a nice gesture by Mr. Hendrix — sending the guitar; but it may have hurt more than helped Jimi. Playing his music, you see, he neglected his duties and eventually had to leave the Army — 'unsuitability,' was the official reason. He was lucky in some ways, though. Before he left the military, he had finished paratrooper training. If he'd stayed in, he might have been killed in Vietnam."

Andrew concluded, "He went on to a great career, then. This was just a bump in the road to a success that was meant to be."

"Well, success and then disaster. You know how unscrupulous promoters and slick agents take advantage of people when they become famous, when they have some money. They made sure he had a ready supply of alcohol and drugs. He died of an overdose in 1971 — about the time I was in Vietnam." It was also the same time his friend had died.

Jonah had prematurely grey hair and wore it in a crisp military cut. His stout physique and square

214

jaw made him look more like an officer than a sergeant, though Harry had a hard time accepting the theory that a sniper had mistaken him for the commander of allied forces in all of Vietnam.

Still, everyone knew the enemy wanted to take out leaders, so a unit's commander might not be positioned at the head of a formation, a primary target. It was widely believed that the life expectancy of second lieutenants taking troops into combat was less than 30 minutes.

"It happens to so many musicians," Donna clucked. "They're troubled souls from the beginning and get into drugs …and other vices."

Harry had to agree. "True, there are a lot of stories like Jimi's—the money and attention go to their heads and they lose all perspective." He rubbed his chin thoughtfully. "Still, though, I'm trying to see the Holy Spirit at work in all this—the time in the Army, the music, the war, the tours, the industry. It must lead to more than a tragic death. Good is supposed to come out of evil, so maybe your good fortune," he nodded at Andrew, "*was* in the making for half a century."

He and Christine glanced at each other.

"It is kind of a high price to be paid, though, when you think about it, to take you two to Las Vegas." Harold hurried on. "I sometimes wonder a lot about what happened to me—you know, being drafted—'selected,' as it were, by *Selective* Service—going to Vietnam, and surviving. I don't think all those other men, on both sides, died so I could

215

have a good life, but it does make me reflect sometimes—and be grateful that I was spared."

Andrew scowled. "God doesn't make wars, men do. It happens all the time in the Bible. People stray from the faith, and they're punished."

"Yes, the Jews were sent into exile. But do you think every one of the Jews was corrupt? I mean, are all the men and women who die in Vietnam, or Iraq, or Afghanistan fallen sinners? Or were their deaths necessary so that God could show the rest of us the errors of our ways?" He shook his head. "Whew! This sort of philosophy or theology or whatever it is is just too complicated for an old man like me."

As Donna went for dessert, he rose and followed her into the kitchen. Ostensibly, he was getting coffee, but also he hoped to give what he'd said time to sink in.

He recalled the morale-boosting tour of General Abrams to units in I Corps. Calculating that the enemy would be unable to mount any kind of attack in the region at this point, the Army publicized the trip widely. Back home—and around the world—the General was seen getting out of helicopters in jungle villages, shaking hands with men in mess halls, telling subordinates in sandbagged headquarters' buildings that peace was near at hand.

Harry and Jonah's CO had all the men's names put in a hat, and he drew out two who would have the good fortune to be among those greeting the

216

general when he visited a firebase near the coast. Due to a mix-up, they were flown in at the same time the General was expected. The first man off the chopper, Jonah, was dropped by a sniper's single bullet fired, they claimed, from a quarter of a mile away. Harry had been right behind his friend. They both had only a week left in their tours.

Harry set coffee at his and Donna's place, knowing the young couple wouldn't want any.

Donna, coming behind him, sang out, "Anyone for dessert?" She carried one of her famous apple pies, hot from the oven.

# Hidden Acres

In the first month with his new (and almost certainly his last) company, Victor established the principle that he ate lunch alone. He explained to his fellow insurance agents that he needed to get away to think in the middle of the day, but the truth was he had quickly tired of their relentless complaints about the decline of America.

When, in his first week, he was invited to join in their mocking of policy statements made by human resources at the national office, he felt he saw the lay of the land ...and he didn't like it.

Martha had pointed to a new memorandum that stated: "'Deceased employees will not be considered for end-of-year bonuses.' Duh!"

"So," Victor asked in all seriousness, "what did you suggest they write instead?"

Dennis brushed him off. "Pointing out the callousness of statements like this would lead to more paragraphs of bureaucratic double-speak. We just disappear this stuff in the cylindrical file beside our desks."

Victor had accepted that answer, but noted the double standard—everyone else always had to know precisely what to say, but this group didn't. Who the hell knew what to say about death anyway?

218

Today the crew found him at the new Chinese Restaurant, Secret Garden, which had opened two blocks from the office. "We can join you this once, can't we, Vic?" asked Martha with the voice that customers found hard to reject.

The restaurant was nearly full, but Victor had been put at a table for four close to the kitchen. He folded a sheet of paper he'd been studying and inserted it between the pages of *Lost Horizons*. Then he waved at the empty chairs, "Sure, sure," while trying to disguise the sigh he made for the friend who, he had just learned, was gone.

Victor hoped they wouldn't continue the topic of conversation they'd been on at coffee break this morning: signs that included misstatements, redundancies, contradictions. "'Gate will open,'" Jack had snarked to start things off. A long-time employee, he was referring to what he read at the exit from the St. Louis airport terminal parking. "Hell. If it won't open, it's a fence, not a gate."

"How about this one?" added Martha, who'd won statewide agent of the month twice the previous year. "The new development south of ours not only has a street named 'Thoroughfare Road,' but there's a crossing street called 'Expressway Trail.' I want to ask a taxi driver to take me to the intersection of those two — or is it four!"

Dennis Smith, hired at the same time as Victor but thirty years younger, chimed in. "I still think the sign in front of the B. D. Mize Funeral Home is too blatant. Couldn't Mr. Mize leave off one initial or spell out either his first or his middle name?"

At the restaurant, Victor could almost predict what would happen if they did return to this theme. When Dennis took a menu from the clip on the napkin ring, his mental prophecy was fulfilled. His colleague pointed at the restaurant's name. "'Secret' Garden? Don't they realize if it were secret, we couldn't find it?" The others giggled and scanned the list of dishes.

Victor decided, if they were imposing on his lunch hour, he could impose on their complacency. "I used to grimace at such unintended messages until I figured out 'Hidden Acres.'"

A server came with additional place settings and took their orders. When he'd gone, Jack asked, "So what was 'Hidden Acres'? A farm or a neighborhood no one could find?"

"RV Campground along the route of my commute in from Pacific. But you get the point: why would you claim a place you want people to come to is a place they can't find?" He paused. "However, I learned to appreciate that name when I realized how many things are, in a sense, 'hidden' right before our eyes."

He almost shivered when he thought about how his friend had covered up the truth about his military past and then hidden his present condition — so much pain.

"I began to understand 'Hidden Acres,'" he

said, "when I was looking at the real estate classifieds in the paper. Has it ever occurred to you as strange that the photos of houses are always taken from the street?"

"No. That's just the way it's done. It says, 'Here's what the house looks like.'"

"True, but you're not giving the potential homeowner the prospect he or she would enjoy if he purchased the house; it's the view others would have of the buyer's home. The picture is that of the outsider, not the insider; yet the idea is to have the purchaser understand what it would be like to live in this house, not outside it."

"I guess this means we're a culture of voyeurs, even of our own lives," laughed Martha.

Victor agreed. "We are certainly a society that looks at itself. Or, put it another way, we study what we want to be in real estate ads, commercials, magazine spreads, book covers."

Their food arrived, so there was a pause while they passed salt, unfolded napkins, picked up utensils. Then Victor continued. "Not only do we ogle romanticized versions of ourselves in the media, but those pictures obscure what we are in fact. We're encouraged to look for certain things, but our attention is also directed away from other things that are equally 'there.'"

"I think I understand; what's hidden in these ads is living room, bedroom, kitchen, etc. — all inside."

221

"Exactly. Now, with internet ads, this is changing, as you can get pictures of different rooms. But still certain views are featured, others hidden."

"Of course, the leaky roof, the creaking stair, the out-of-date wiring. Still, I don't feel confused by all this. Most of us know to read between the lines, get an official inspection." Dennis signaled the server for more tea.

"Okay, but here's an example of how we do this to ourselves without realizing it." Victor pulled a crumbled paper napkin from his pocket and held it in one hand. "I have two regular jogging routes (as well as some other irregular ones): summer and winter. In both it turns out I blinded myself to an entire house."

"You must have been looking the other way every time you passed."

"Yes and no. First, let me explain why the two routes. Since I love the outdoors, from April to October I run through my neighborhood and then out on a country road, passing a few scattered houses, cows, fields. This is my preferred way. But when daylight hours began to shorten in the fall, I have to trade it for an in-town one."

"As a bicyclist, I understand," offered Jack. "It's too hard for motorists to see you in that season, even with reflective gear; and the potholes are hard to spot."

"People also tend to see only car-sized vehicles,

not bikes or motorcycles or pedestrians. So, running, I crisscross a dozen blocks in town, looking at homes, yards, athletic fields, sometimes illuminated by streetlights. Same distance, same time, but different path. Of course, I'm a lot slower than I used to be, but the cardiovascular benefits still outweigh the aches and pains. If you saw me, you might claim I was just walking fast."

He took a long sip of his water, and they understood they had just heard the exposition. The plot would thicken, but he wasn't sure if he'd take them through the running and on to the collapse.

"Now, on the summer route the last house I pass on my way out of town is a small brick home. Its modest front stoop, wide dining room or living room window, small kitchen or bath window face Oak Street. I have always imagined two bedrooms and a bath behind them. As many runners do, of course, I mainly register the house in my vision, not inspect it or analyze it in any detail. It's more a landmark that tells me I've finished the first leg of my run."

Martha suggested. "Something hidden there, I bet, which you discovered late one night chasing your dog, who'd slipped through the fence (not a gate!). A secret gambling club, a moonshine factory, a madame and her 'girls.'"

"It's not as dramatic as that, but, yes, there is something hidden. But I need to describe the winter run to uncover it. From October to April I turn off Oak one block short of that last little brick

223

home. I run south for a shortened block on Apple, then turn west on the street parallel to Oak — Elm Street. Down Elm past three houses for one block, turn south again, continue on my way in town, not out of town."

"I can imagine the neighborhood in that small, former railroad town. Little two-bedroom homes, small lots, but still kept up quite well."

"Pretty accurate; modest houses in neat rows." Victor decided not to mention that Dennis could picture the homes because he had absorbed the stock images from television, movies, newspapers. He wondered if he should pull out the letter he tucked inside his book.

He went on. "Elm and Oak are so close together that each lot stretches across the intervening space between the two parallel streets. There's one house per lot facing Oak and backing up to Elm."

"If there are a lot of houses and they look much the same, I could see how you might never notice one."

"Here's how I finally discovered it." He noticed that Martha was signaling the server. "Oh, are you having dessert?"

She only wanted the check, so Victor continued. "Remember: in the winter my landmark Oak Street house presents to passersby like me on Elm its bedroom windows on the back of the structure."

"Ah, one day you learned from the back view that it was actually a mob hideout, a CIA safe house, a woman who keeps thirty cats."

"I'm beginning to fear this is going to be anticlimactic. But anyway, not so long ago—after about two decades of following this route—I looked at the little brick house on Elm and saw a front stoop, a wide window for living or dining room, a small window for kitchen or bath. How could this be? This was the *back* of my Oak Street house."

"You must have been confused about where you were and were looking at a different home."

"No. In fact, I ran another block before I was able to take this in. I should have seen bedroom windows appropriate to the back of the house, not windows and a stoop that belonged to a front. So, how can the house on Oak have two fronts?"

"Omigosh! There are two houses."

"That's it. When I retraced my steps and realized—well, I knew it all along but had never let it take shape in my mind—that, as Elm and Oak proceed west, they diverge—from half a block apart at Apple Street to a full block apart. The first two houses I pass after turning off Apple to go down Elm present their backs, but not the third. In other words, at the western end of that block there are two lots/houses in the place where I had thought there was only one."

He pulled out the napkin he'd tucked into his

225

pocket when they came to his table and spread it out before them. It had a sketch of the neighborhood he'd been talking about.

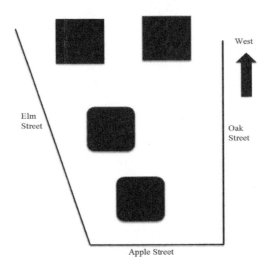

He turned the drawing around so they could see it from his perspective. As they studied it, the server brought the check on a little tray with four fortune cookies.

Jack leaned in and said. "There were also two front yards and two backyards, not one of each. How could you have missed that ...um, that 'hidden' house?"

"For a good while I was embarrassed to be so unobservant, so blind. But then I began to turn my experience into something positive. Rather than being disappointed at this discovery, I celebrated the fact that my world had just expanded. Now I

226

had two houses where for decades there had been only one. There were also, as you indicated, two front yards and two backyards. My world was richer than I'd ever known!" He broke open his fortune cookie.

"But no underground neo-Nazi party, no pot-smoking hippie commune, no militant religious sect with enough firepower and provisions to hold off the FBI for a month?"

"Not a bit. Just another regular family, same as the ones all of us grew up in and of which we are now the next generation."

"Ah, so we've hidden the fact that there may be twice as many of us as we thought," concluded Dennis. "Duplicates as far as the eye can see."

Victor turned his pen over and over in one hand. "Yeah."

Then he took a sheet of paper from the copy of *Lost Horizons* he'd been reading when they had all come over to his table. He'd gone this far; he might as well go all the way. The sheet was folded in half and then in thirds, the way a letter would be to fit in a small envelope. "Take a look at this and see what you think it means."

They could all view it at the same time, and the handwriting was small but easy to read.

Victor Whiskey,

Good to hear from you. Brought back old times.

Got to see the kids weekend before last. Wow, had they grown! Linda looks good, too, though I could see the strain my being there caused her. Still, I felt I had the right, know what I mean? Anyway, it was hard to say this goodbye.

I've got a new guy from the VA helping me. He knows the deal. Everything continues trés bien with me

If you come up to Omaha one day, I'll show you around. I miss seeing you, even though it's been …what? a decade. Hug the wife and the kids.

There was a neat signature, "Charlie Dog," at the bottom.

"'Whiskey' is your middle name?" asked Martha. "And he's Charlie Dog? That's a bit strange."

"Those are nicknames. He is Charlie, but somewhere along the way we added the military alphabet codes. Everybody gets renamed in the Army." He didn't present his own theory that the Army liked the informal practice of re-naming because it gave everyone a non-civilian identity. And real names made it harder when someone bought it.

"I didn't know you were a vet."

"Army draftee, quite a few years ago. We tend to keep a low profile."

"Huh. Okay, what are we supposed to see in the letter? I mean, this Charlie's having a hard a

228

time—divorced, I guess, but getting counseling. Do you need us to help you write a response?"

"No, no response is necessary." A pause. "He won't ever read it."

Now they were the ones who paused. Then Jack asked, "Is he …gone?"

"Right. This is a suicide note, but …but the clue is hidden. Well, it was right there in front of me, but remained invisible all the same. Or maybe I didn't want to see it."

"Oh, my," said Martha. "Instead of there being another one of you—like the extra house you discovered—there's just empty space somewhere in Omaha, Nebraska."

Victor agreed. "And no one will discover the Charlie Dog I used to know, the one who survived the war but not the peace. I'm not even sure Linda knew all he had been through, though she did the best of anyone back here, bless her."

"I guess you'd better tell us what you missed in the letter, what's hidden here. Or is it a code only someone who'd been in the military would recognize?" Victor could tell Jack would prefer the whole conversation be abandoned.

He shrugged. "Well, the 'this' before the 'goodbye' makes it distinctive." He pointed to the passage. "But—and you wouldn't know this—but *trés bien* must be his code for Ben Tre, a village where bad things happened."

"My Lai kinds of things?"

"Something like that, though not intentional. Charlie had hidden what we saw there from everyone back here."

"Ah, so he was not 'very well.'"

"No. I thought it was odd that he used a French phrase, even a common one. It's …it *wasn't* like him, a conventional Midwesterner like me. But I read over it, passed it by."

He looked down at the little slip of paper with his fortune printed out: "*A home that welcomes all is seldom seen.*"

They couldn't find anything to say, so Victor looked at his watch. "Holy cow! We'd better get back to work! Got to fill out forms and file papers."

At his desk he tried to do just that, but the letter from Charlie wouldn't let him. The past— behind the hand that penned the words inscribed on the letter tucked into the book carried under his arm—had been loosed on another man cursed to have once seen a village, a street, a house. Victor watched the rockets, heard the explosions, smelled the burning. But not the way his friend had.

Tomorrow Victor would drive to Kansas City where Private First Class Charles Oscar Golf, Mortuary Affairs Specialist (92M), would be buried. He would see his friend one last time.

# The Soy Bean Field

Sharon heard her husband telling the guests, "Our cocker spaniels have no street sense," and wondered what event he had kept hidden from her. Louis often took the sisters, twins from the same litter, with him to their Bootheel house. Perhaps they had gotten away from him, and he hadn't told her about it.

"You've always walked them on a leash here, right?" their guest Debbie assumed. "And I saw you have a fence out back." She was a junior staff member in the Environmental Geology Office, new this fall to the Survey and the area.

"Right, but I've read about the breed, and, while they can find birds by their scent, they have no idea where they've been or where they are in relationship to a starting point. Just lost in a field."

And that was Sharon's clue that he was about to slide into his one Vietnam story. How this occasion required it, she couldn't guess. Sometimes he started his account of going A.W.O.L. and couldn't finish it.

"I can be like that, not sure where I've been or where I'm going," joked Thomas, Debbie's husband, who had just been hired as an assistant loan manager at Fairfield State Bank. "But sometimes I deliberately keep where I've been a secret."

"Don't think I don't have my spies, darling," Debbie said, her head tilted back; but Sharon felt her smile was forced. The town of Fairfield was still small enough that marital indiscretions were hard to hide. And a man as good-looking as Thomas was noticed.

Sharon had caught an undertone in Debbie's conversation earlier that suggested the couple's relationship might be under strain. A hospital chaplain, she knew the stress two professional careers can put on a marriage when one partner, especially a man, feels the sacrifice is all on one side. She understood that Louis' fidelity to her was grounded in her having waited for him during his overseas tour.

Louis went on. "We have this river house down near Sikeston, southeast corner of the state." Even though Debbie now worked for the state Division of Geological Land Survey, he felt he should explain where this was because she and Thomas were Illinois natives. "We spend a lot of our summers there, but I also go down periodically in the winter just to make sure everything's secure—no water flowing from broken pipes, mold not taking over the closets, squirrels kept from getting into the attic and eating the wiring."

The house was over one hundred years of age, and they were in the process of modernizing it as a retirement home. They both loved houses that had stood the test of time, but knew regular maintenance was even more important than in modern constructions. Sharon was often busy on weekends, and wasn't able to take the three-hour trip down as frequently as he, senior head of the Water Tracing Department. Louis didn't mind, convinced he was keeping his peace of mind by regular escapes to their hideaway.

"I hope it's in a more lively place than Fairfield," observed Thomas. "This burg closes up at 6:00, even on weekends."

Sharon agreed. "We are a family-oriented community. A lot of our entertainment is having friends over for dinner, as tonight." She swept a hand in front of her to include them all in the evening. Looking at Louis, she smiled, "He doesn't do it just because he's the boss."

"Princess and the Queen thought they wanted more excitement, too," said Louis, steering the conversation back to the dogs. "When they escaped the PT Cruiser, they were ready to chase other dogs, stray cats, field mice. But they discovered a truth I learned forty years ago." Sharon could tell he was already seeing the Mekong Delta rice field in his memory, the rows of young stalks, women in conical hats knee deep in the water, permanent low hanging clouds in the rainy season. And then the jungle.

"Let me freshen your drinks," Sharon said, smiling. "This might take a while."

"Can I help?" asked Debbie, half rising from the sofa.

"Oh, no. The lasagna just has fifteen more minutes in the oven; the salad's already made." She grinned. "And he needs an audience."

Thomas took a long pull on his beer. Sharon saw it as another sign of the restless spouse caught in a social engagement with the partner's professional associates. In the kitchen, still able to hear her husband, she recalled the discomfort she had felt initially at the Survey's social events. She checked on the lasagna, wondering when Louis would start his story about taking a stroll off base.

"The girls ride in the back, with the seats down flat, behind a gate. And generally they fall asleep once I'm under way. But this time, Queen—who's the Alpha dog, as you might guess from her name—was restless. Maybe she smelled the cookies I had stashed away. Anyway, she pawed the gate in some way, and it fell back on top of both dogs."

"And they were in the front seat with you in a flash, weren't they?" laughed Debbie. When she'd met the cocker spaniels earlier, kneeling down to accept their eager tongues, she explained how she'd always had dogs, at least until she married.

"You're right. And I'm trucking down a two-lane road at 55 miles per hour, so I'll have to stop to put the gate back. This is all flatland, nothing but fields around me. But then I spot a farm road—really, just two tire tracks in the dirt—and pull in."

"This isn't going to be a *Deliverance* story, is it?" asked Thomas, though his expression was hopeful. "Or something about a meth lab hidden in the

234

woods?"

Debbie had told Louis that her husband, having lived all his life in big cities, had not been eager to come to what he characterized with the expression, "not the end of the earth—but you can see it from there." Still, like some people from other areas he was intrigued by the wild tales of hillbilly decadence in films like *Winter's Bone*. Did such things really happen, a girl sawing off her father's hands?

"My story isn't nearly so dramatic, though," assured Louis. "As you'll see in a moment, I could have been killed if human nature—well, if *canine* nature hadn't asserted itself. See, I found I couldn't get their fence back up while I was in the front seat; I was going to have to go around, open the tailgate, and put it in place. So, I pointed a stern finger at Royalty—that's their collective name—told them, 'stay,' and backed out of the driver's side door."

Again, Debbie was quick to pick up. "They got past you."

"Call of the wild," suggested Thomas, looking at the window as if he'd like to follow some primitive instinct out into the night.

"It may have been simple curiosity, but, you're right. First Queen was on the ground, then Princess followed. I caught the second one by her rear end, though. She is a sweet dog, the subservient one, and will let me do anything to her. So, I pitched her back in and turned to find Queen."

"Not in the road, I hope?"

"On the shoulder, but, fortunately, nose to the ground. And bless the Lord, there were no cars coming either way." He paused. Sharon, taking her time in the kitchen to let Louis have center stage, heard him lower his voice conspiratorially and imagined him leaning in: "If she'd been in the road, and a car coming, I knew I might as well lie down there with her. Queen is Sharon's dog. If she were run over, I would have said, 'Take me, too, Jesus. Take me now.'"

They both laughed, though Thomas seemed unsure if he should. Debbie said, "If I had a dog, and Thomas lost her, …he'd better pray, too."

"Maybe that's why I don't want any pets. Besides, we might be moving next year, if I get an offer I can't refuse."

Debbie had confided in Louis about Thomas' restlessness. He'd taken the Fairfield bank job more as a holding action than a commitment, and Debbie feared he would later ask her to give up her position and follow him.

Sharon carried the drink refills in on a tray, and Louis went on with the story. "So, when Queen stopped …to do what dogs do, to leave her mark, so to speak …I pounced on her." He paused, anticipating chuckles. "I was polite, though, and let her finish."

Thomas tried to continue the story, "Then you turned around and were face-to-face with a wolf, or

236

a pack of wolves."

Louis laughed. Sharon raised her eyebrows as she handed another beer to Thomas, more sparkling water to Debbie.

"No wolves," admitted Louis. "But the danger wasn't over. I got her back to the car, plunked her down on the front seat so I could fix the gate."

"She didn't get away again?" asked Sharon.

"She did! Sly fox, right between my legs. But this time she went away from the road, out into the field."

Sharon suspected Thomas's personal experience could produce no picture of a soy bean field in late fall: the plants about eighteen inches tall, dark green leaves, parallel rows down the rich, sandy, delta soil. Nor would this young couple be able to envision the rice paddies, the water buffalo, the twin buckets carried across the shoulders Louis had described for her. That's what he had passed on that day he wandered away from his base, a moment of madness on a day of sorrow.

"Again, I kept Princess in the car and went after her sister. She'd gone about ten yards or so down the path, then turned into the soy beans."

Sharon added. "If you've never seen them, it's a pretty site in the fall. The fields are completely flat, so the rows are straight and go as far as a mile sometimes."

"That's right," agreed Louis. "And Queen was

prancing down between two rows, her cocker spaniel ears flopping, her nose up to smell the air. All I could do was play defense, like a basketball player: stay between the other player and the goal behind me."

"The goal being the road in this case," said Debbie.

"Yes. I figured she could go as far as she wanted into the field. I just had to keep her from being flattened by a speeding car."

Thomas wondered. "Maybe there was a boy dog out there on the prowl, tired of the monogamous life, looking to score. Know what I mean? You might have ended up with a litter of mongrel pups."

"Thomas," said Debbie softly.

Louis answered, "That would have been one of my worries, if she hadn't been spayed. But, as I said earlier, canine nature kicked in. Or something pretty deep inside her."

In her mind, Sharon heard Louis' account of passing through the fence of the base near Can Tho, walking past rice fields, wandering into a clump of banana trees. The branches arched over the path, blocking the sun, and he found himself standing in what was almost a tunnel or a cave. He became aware of flitting shadows, unpleasant smells, strange animal (and human?) sounds. The insane impulse to desert, to find the river, to escape by boat, evaporated.

"I know we can't read a dog's mind," Louis admitted. "Shoot, we can't even put their thoughts into our words, but still, that day I felt I knew what Queen was thinking."

"Oh?"

"You see, what happened was, all of a sudden, Queen stopped where she was and looked around her—ahead, to this side, to that. She had to stretch her neck to see over the soy bean plants, they were that tall then. She was the picture of alertness, scouting the territory before making a dash for whatever interested her most."

Thomas again interjected, "I'm telling you, some wild dog, who wouldn't care if another dog was in heat or not, …"

"Thomas!" This time Debbie's voice was louder, and sharper.

Louis hurried on as if they had not spoken. "One moment Queen was free, the world open all around her; she could escape all barriers, do whatever she wanted. Then she froze. And I am honestly convinced she thought something like, 'I have never in my life seen anything that remotely resembles this. Where the hell am I? There are no sidewalks here, no front lawns, not a house in sight. This is an alien landscape, a foreign world.'"

Debbie agreed. "I can understand that—a town dog out in the country."

"And I tell you, she looked around, and then she looked back at me. I'm about ten rows toward

239

the road, again ready to intercept her if she comes this way. She looks at me, and I am certain she thinks: 'Hmm, I know that guy, that guy yelling at me to get back here. He keeps me on a leash and makes me walk in the yard and takes me to the vet, but …but, you know, he also gives me food and belly rubs. I understand him. Out here,' she says to herself, again looking around, 'it's weird. I don't know how this place works. And I don't trust it.'"

"You mean that she came back to you on her own?" Debbie smiled.

"You've got it exactly. She took one last glance around her, then turned and trotted back down the row to the double tire tracks (where I'd moved too in a parallel fashion, still playing defense), came right up to me, and let me swoop her up, plunk her back in the car."

Thomas said, "Ah, she bailed. Took the easy way out." He finished his beer. "So many do that."

Debbie opened her mouth to speak, but Sharon took the cue. "Well, I think that it's a happy ending to a shaggy dog story, so, please, let's all come to the table."

Debbie and Thomas excused themselves to wash their hands after petting dogs, and perhaps recover some social composure. Sharon sent a worried glance after the young couple and raised her eyebrows to Louis. He shrugged. She suspected he wasn't going to make the transition into his Vietnam story after all.

Sharon knew Louis hadn't told his story many times, seldom certain it was the right occasion. And his tour as a map compiler was uneventful except for this one incident, so he had no traditional war story full of daring and courage to offer. It didn't cast him in a great role either, oblivious of the people they'd supposedly come to protect and liberate, abandoning those who depended on him.

True, on the morning of his stroll, Louis had watched them bag the bodies of two men blown to pieces when a rocket landed in their bunker. Choppered in the day before to gather updated intelligence maps, he'd drunk beer with Duke and Roy while waiting for the ride out that didn't come. They had gone on perimeter guard duty, and he sacked out in their hootch. The shells came with the first light of dawn. What Louis, standing in a clump of banana trees, later understood at an almost visceral level seemed to be so important he struggled for ways and places to communicate it.

When they were all seated, Sharon asked with a smile, "So Debbie, tell me what it's like to work for my husband?"

"Don't answer that," Louis laughed, but she did.

# Counterinsurgency

At the after-church, pot-luck luncheon Adam listened to the young psychologist talk about his research into "trust-building in counterinsurgency efforts." A Vietnam veteran, Adam remembered the famous chicken pho prepared by the hootch's mama-sans and wondered if it had ever occurred to him or anyone in his unit that they were supposed to "build trust" through that meal.

"The American military is facing a new kind of war," explained Jason, newly hired assistant professor at St. Mary's College. "We don't have tanks on one side facing tanks on another."

This man was so young, Adam thought, Vietnam must seem ancient history to him. But the retired insurance agent had already concluded his generation's war was a past from which America hadn't learned. We were doomed to repeat errors in such places as Iraq and Afghanistan.

"I see," he offered thoughtfully. "So the enemy look like civilians and vice versa, eh?"

"Exactly. And we won't know who the bad guys are unless we establish a solid relationship with the good guys."

"Ah. And the, uh, the military is interested in your research?" The Army's Fort A. P. Hill was a little more than an hour away.

"Well, they *are* helping to fund it." He sipped his herbal tea and grinned. "You see, we've built up a mutual trust."

Adam didn't see much trust between military and civilian these days, more a willingness to turn over the job of protecting United States interests around the world to those still moved by patriotism and those desperate for a job. So long as our comfortable lifestyle was preserved, no questions were asked back home.

Forty some years ago, civilians were openly antagonistic to the military, spitting on soldiers returning from Vietnam and calling them baby killers. He recalled no "invite a vet to dinner" program.

When he had been stationed in Long Binh, Adam was one of thousands of U.S. soldiers whose trust building with the people of South Vietnam was conducted via a handful of pidgin English phrases. "Two cartons Marlboro, you wash," created a contract for a woman to clean uniforms in tubs set up by the showers. Closer to the gates, one could hear offers from the men who sold goods in tin huts just outside the base: "You want girl, GI? Cameras, watches, dope?" And on payday trips to the Chinese restaurant (run by Koreans) soldiers would say, "No want chop sticks, okay?"

Several men in his outfit, mostly draftees, took a casual interest in Vietnamese life, perhaps trying to create a social environment that wasn't completely military. That's how the idea originated that the two mama-sans who worked in the area should cook for the men (not that many really wanted to eat their food). It was the inspiration of The Reverend Norfolk.

"Norfolk" Bobby Turner earned his second nickname by launching into a "come to Jesus" sermon one Sunday during a dawn rocket attack. He started softly in the bunker, urging repentance from those sins that would throw them all into the burning flames of hell. He sang the refrain from "Just as I Am." No one could tell if he was mocking, serious, or mentally unstable.

"We'll break bread with them, guys," he explained after he'd offered Mama-san one of the ten-dollar bills his girlfriend was hiding in the letters she sent him. Soldiers could only use script or piastres in-country; green was traded on the black market. "You know, sit down to eat with 'em, a family affair."

Tex (who was from Oklahoma) said he wasn't eating their food. "Man, they shovel in whatever it is they eat with their fingers. My nose says it mostly rotten fish."

"There's dog in there, I tell you," claimed Raymond from somewhere near Dover, Delaware. "They catch the little ones on base, strangle them, and carry them out hidden in their baskets. The MPs look the other way."

Adam decided to feed his paranoia. "Look out for tiny bamboo punji sticks covered in shit. You won't even notice while you're eating, but they'll

244

slice open your stomach. If you don't bleed through your asshole overnight, infection will kill you in a couple of days. Dead, Little Ray, either way."

"It can't be worse than the mess hall," claimed The Reverend and added sanctimoniously: "I'll bless the food."

"I'm game," said Wilson, the most educated of the group. "You meatheads might even learn something."

Wilson had studied Vietnamese at the Army's language school in California; but, ignoring his nine months of training, the Army made him a diet therapy steward over here. In-country, they used nationals (who wanted to learn English) as translators rather than their own troops. Wilson had helped pay for his education by working at the Johns Hopkins cafeteria, so he was attached to the mess hall.

The night before the event Adam drank too much at the E-5 club. He nearly lost what was left in his stomach staggering out of the hootch the next morning on his way to the latrine. Mama-san had just wrung a chicken's neck, chopped its head off, and was letting it run in circles on the sand. The men, none of whom had been in the bush, laughed nervously.

She plucked the bird, cut it up with a knife (no one knew how she'd gotten that blade through security!), and put the heart, gizzard, undeveloped eggs, and some bones in a pot to cook over Sterno cans. A cloth bag full of spices was added and, after

245

a few hours, white rice noodles.

With a bit of "the hair of a dog," Adam got control of his system, but he didn't find the simmering dish appetizing, especially as mama-san kept skimming fat and other unidentifiable bits off the top. Still, he took some in his mess kit cup, pretended to like it, then slipped outside to pour it on the other side of the sandbag wall.

Forty years later, sitting opposite Jason the psychologist at a conference table in the church parish house, he reconsidered the whole affair. "Do you think sharing a meal with the indigenous people is a good idea?" he asked.

"Absolutely. That's what military advisors are trained to do today, get to know the people and their customs. You have to live among them."

"Now that you say that, I guess state dinners for visiting dignitaries are sort of the same thing."

"That's right," agreed Jason. "Of course," he added, holding up an "extra crispy" drumstick, "for prime ministers, presidents, and dictators, we try to do a little better than Kentucky Fried — American though it is."

Adam smiled and looked around at the gathering, perhaps fifty parishioners of all ages. The new priests, a couple, wanted to have at least one social event like this each month. The old-timers, very traditional Episcopalians, had resisted at first, just as they thought having communion every Sunday was excessive. But they were trying to be accommodating to the young people—building trust without knowing it, Adam concluded now.

He thought back to his Army training. During basic at Fort Bragg, North Carolina, had he been told anything about understanding the people of South Vietnam? Perhaps there were lectures on their traditions, their customs, their cuisine? Like most of the other recruits, he had dozed through too many of those sessions.

Only two things stood out now. First was a diagram of how, if you were lost in the jungle, you could catch a monkey for food with a shiny object and a hollowed out coconut shell. Second was the life-size cardboard figure of a Viet Cong. The fake Charlie—infamous "Victor Charles"—wore the iconic black pajamas, sandals, conical hat—and was holding an AK-47. Had Adam been supposed to ask the original out to eat? It seemed more that he was supposed to shoot him on sight.

Jason went on, "As you know, hospitality is an element of many traditions. Take the Greeks. Poor wandering Odysseus, trying to get home to Penelope, measures the nature of each group he encounters by how they treat strangers."

"Yes, the Cyclops spit their guests on poles, roast them over the fire, and eat them. Not high on the list of good guys."

"The truth can come out on such occasions, too. Judas was at the Last Supper and then betrayed Christ."

Adam recalled one more scene from the chicken pho feast: Wilson, "The Brain," talking quietly with mama-san as she cleaned up. What were Mama-san and Wilson saying, Adam wondered four decades later? Were they comparing memories from their different childhoods, their hopes for the future? Were they seeking common ground in their disparate traditions, America and Vietnam? Could Adam somehow replay that scene in his mind and enter the conversation? Unlikely.

But maybe Jason and his colleagues could. Who knew? The world was, as they'd sung in the '60s, a-changin'. Why not bet on trust? His generation seemed to have lost it; perhaps the next would recover it.

# The West Texas Wave

"Do you realize today is the 35-year anniversary of the day I was drafted?" Ted asked his wife of 34 years, eleven months, fourteen days.

"Is it?" Felicia said. "In a lot of ways, it doesn't seem that long ago."

"Yeah."

In fact, that was the scary part: more and more events now were recalling things that had happened then. And some were troubling.

"Let's concentrate on our first vacation without children," Fel said. "Without work worries, without the pressure of deadlines."

The Youngs had decided to take a month off this year and drive leisurely west, stopping on whim and staying when they could with friends. They'd just spent a surprisingly pleasant evening in a quiet B & B north of Tulsa. Ted had wanted to get off the beaten path of interstates now and then, traveling some of the older two-lane roads.

"This must have been what Route 66 was like fifty years ago," he told Felicia as they drove north off I-44. "Cement road with tar-patched cracks. But you got to see the land, meet the people."

"Yes, John Steinbeck's 'The Mother Road,' part of America's forgotten history. You know, though, at our age I prefer traveling without surprises, even if it means staying in chain motels. Or at B & B's we've thoroughly researched on the Internet."

"Okay, but remember you're also the one who wanted to see a forgotten piece of the nation's landscape."

The B & B they'd left that morning was close to one of the last natural stands of tallgrass prairie in the country. A century and more ago, thousands of square miles had been plowed under as settlers moved west to homestead, but a recent effort to protect remaining portions was gaining momentum. Felicia taught botany and plant communities at Hermann College in Virginia; and the survival of species in distinct habitats intrigued her, especially when so many plants were threatened now by rapid environmental change.

"I've wanted to see such a sight for years," she explained. Ted had been surprised himself at the scene — peaceful, solitary, simple.

The next morning, as they continued toward San Angelo, Texas, where their former pastor and his wife were living, Ted admitted, "You know, sitting out on the plains for two hours last night was a pretty good way to show we've escaped routine."

"You want to tell me what you learned about the natural world?" Before they had driven out there after supper, she gave Ted a short lecture on biodiversity, habitat fragmentation and loss, invasive plant species like eastern red cedar.

"Hmm. You would know what grasses or bushes or reeds were hiding along the stream," admitted Ted. "But I did see some neat birds." He paused. "That one eastern meadowlark singing his heart out on the end of a branch was kind of sad."

She looked over at him. "You're not letting that hitchhiker bother you, are you?"

On their way out of Springfield, a man in worn desert fatigues and an incongruous bright yellow scarf had been raising a thumb half-heartedly, as if confident no one would offer to help a veteran in distress. Ted hadn't, though his left hand did lift off the steering wheel in a partial gesture of recognition. The memory disturbed him because they were likely headed in the same direction, along the path the Joad family had traveled in *The Grapes of Wrath*.

Ted lied to Fel. "The vet by the side of the road? No, I'm not thinking of him. What could we do? Still, I do see stories in the news about homeless vets, vets who can't navigate the VA, too many suicides. Somebody should be doing something."

"What do you suppose the temperature is out there?" Fel cracked a window but rolled it back up quickly. "Another day over 100, I bet."

The month-long hot spell was the lead story on the local news the night before. Ted had wanted to raise their body temperatures in the four-poster on the second floor of an elegant old frame house. But his wife, sensitive to heat, had not been feeling

251

well. "Take a cold shower," she suggested. He grumped; but, married for as long as they had been, he knew better than to complain. She'd jump his bones as soon as she felt better.

"Not that many hours to go" he asserted, though he knew it would get hotter until nightfall. He pushed their speed up close to 80. Felicia, a town person from a green state, would never feel at home in this semi-arid landscape of scattered, stunted mesquite and few hills.

Ted was thinking about the veteran, though, recalling how he himself had hitchhiked to all sorts of places in Vietnam as an Army correspondent. He had on green jungle fatigues, not the dull, sandy brown, desert ones worn by soldiers from Iraq and Afghanistan. Any military vehicle—jeep, truck, personnel carrier—from any nation—America, Australia, South Korea, the Philippines—would give him a lift. And his Army press card would get him on air shuttles, choppers, cargo planes. Who was picking up the latest generation of warriors?

"You do realize there's nobody out here." Fel was looking ahead, to the left and the right. "We've left civilization behind."

"There are cattle here and there. Must be ranches, ranch houses." To himself he admitted that no people or buildings were in sight.

There was an edge to her response. "Point to one."

He scanned left and right. Then he nodded

straight ahead. "Right there." There was a pick-up truck perhaps a quarter mile in front of them.

The empty landscape made him recall that time he'd gone after a story at a Navy supply base up close to the DMZ …what had he titled it, "The Forgotten Man of …Somewhere"? He'd interviewed a dispatcher who directed cargo in and out of the port. A solitary clerk on a tiny rocky island in the bay, he was a nameless voice to hundreds of Navy boat captains. Once he'd gotten them into port or out to sea, he was history.

Ted realized he was gaining quickly on the little truck ahead. It was probably a farm vehicle driven by some local rancher. Switching on the left turn signal, Ted pulled into the ongoing lane to pass; no other traffic was visible for as far as the eye could see. As he went by, the truck driver moved to the road's paved shoulder, not slowing down.

"That's odd," Ted noted. "Why did he slide over there?"

The shoulder was wide and paved, though slanting down toward the surrounding fields. He suspected the roadway was elevated to preserve it from flooding during heavy spring rains. And the broad asphalt shoulder protected the bed from wash.

He hit the turn blinker, slid into the right lane, glanced up at his rearview mirror. The truck, never changing speeds, pulled up from the shoulder. He clucked his tongue. "For a moment, Fel, no one was

253

where we were supposed to be: I was in the lane for oncoming traffic, he was on the shoulder. Weird!"

"Are we there yet?"

Ted had asked the forgotten man of wherever it was if he felt disconnected at his post, on duty day and night but never seeing the men he was directing face to face. The specialist explained. "Those of us who've been here a while have developed a code." He was on his second tour, which made Ted wonder even more how he stood his isolation.

Out of the corner of his eye, he could see that Fel was uncomfortable. He was beginning to feel the heat himself, and the landscape remained bleak. They were even out of range for anything but country music, which she wouldn't like, on the radio.

When they had passed the hitchhiking vet, Ted had his window down, feeling the cool air of early morning. He thought he heard the veteran whistling a melancholy tune. Had it been a signal? Should he have recognized it?

In the distance he saw two cars approaching, one behind the other. They were so far off that they didn't seem to be moving, just shimmering in the heat on the horizon. Watching a few moments, he realized that the one behind was gaining and would probably pass the one in front.

As if he were watching a movie scene shot

254

with a telescopic lens, he saw the second car close on the leader. Before the driver behind might have pulled into his oncoming lane (the one Ted and Fel were in), the car in front slid down the shoulder on the other side. The trailing car passed him; and the former leader-become-follower pulled up from the shoulder into the regular lane for cars going in their direction.

"That's what they do in West Texas!" said Ted, more to himself than to Fel. "There's not enough traffic out here to justify a four-lane highway; but, with good shoulders, passers can move forward even if people are coming the other way. Cool."

"Cool?" questioned Fel. "I don't think anything's *not* hot around here. Are we coming up to someplace—a town, a village, a crossroads? I could use a cold drink."

"Soon, soon. Maybe you can catch a nap." She slumped down in her seat.

Ted was excited about his discovery, how to pass or be passed in West Texas. Imperceptibly (he hoped), he slowed down. He wanted someone to come up from behind so he could show that he knew the rules of the road out here. He would show he belonged.

It was a risky maneuver inside the car, he knew. Fel would be irritated if she recognized he was not doing all he could to get her to San Angelo quickly. And, as can happen in even the strongest marriage, a small issue can open old, big fissures.

"What code?" Ted had asked Forgotten Man back in Vietnam. "How did you make connections beyond the official military exchanges, the 'Roger that,' 'Copy that,' the 'Over and Out'?"

Forgotten Man had laughed. "We borrowed some CB phrases from our past lives. You know a lot of us were draftees, civilians really, doing our bit. And, if you had been in transportation, you'd learned the lingo."

"Ah. So you used trucker talk. Give me some examples." Ted had a portable tape recorder for this story in addition to the standard spiral notebook. He could do print, audio, or both, depending on the material. With the fog horns, sea sounds, and bird cries recalling a lighthouse keeper's environment, he had already decided he wanted to do a radio feature.

"'Alice in Wonderland' was a ship off course. Any threat was a 'Bogie.' If speed was an issue, you said 'Drop the Hammer Down.' You could usually figure it out from the situation, basically common sense. But we created links outside the system, reminding each other of The World, another life, who we'd been."

Ted checked his rearview mirror. Good luck: someone was gaining. He slowed a bit more, ready to accommodate himself to local customs.

At the appropriate moment, he slid down on the shoulder, trying not to act as if this were unusual even when Fel's head came up and she looked around. The car behind didn't change lanes but passed right by on his left. Smiling, Ted pulled back up into the right lane. Through the rear window of the car in front, he saw the other driver glance up at his rearview mirror, raise his right hand, and give a short, crisp wave.

"Aha!" Ted said out loud. To himself he thought, "I did it. And he knows it."

"What?" asked Fel.

Ted explained what he'd learned, gradually getting the car back to the appropriate speed even though it meant he kept a consistent distance behind the car that had passed them. All she said was, "Get me to John and Nancy's before I get really sick."

He wanted to go fast now for two reasons: to relieve Fel, of course; but also to give what he deemed in his head "the West Texas Wave." If he could pass one more car, make the wave, he would prove that he, New England transplant moved to the South, had joined the community of Westerners who wore cowboy hats, had shotguns in the back of their truck cabs, and could lasso a calf for branding.

Again, fortune smiled on him. After about thirty minutes, another car appeared over a small rise ahead. He pushed the Chrysler four-cylinder family mini-van as hard as it would go. He thought about giving a light tap on the horn when he got close, following a lesson from high school's driver education years ago. But he knew about road range and would rather count on the other driver's being

257

alert to what was behind him.

Soon they came up on a dusty Volvo station wagon. Ted kept the accelerator down, the car ahead slipped onto the shoulder, and they passed the fellow traveler ...well, travelers. There was a passenger in the front seat and what appeared to be sleeping children in the back. Ted watched the driver/father pull up behind him, then raised his right hand and gave the short wave in his mirror. Although he couldn't see the face of the Volvo driver, he was confident there was a quiet acknowledgment in his eyes. He, Ted, had done it. He was a West Texan!

Why, then, when he recounted the event to his old friends that night in their refreshing outdoor swimming pool, did it seem so anti-climatic? Had he told it wrong? Did he leave something out? Could he have somehow missed the point of his own tale?

Their friends confirmed that, yes, that's how they passed in West Texas. But John wandered back in the conversation to the Eastern Meadowlark with its bright yellow underbelly. Birders, they'd added it to their life list in their first year in San Angelo. And they noted how its melancholy call was so recognizable that they had never become deaf to its presence.

Fel, a gin and tonic in the cup holder of her inflated plastic raft, had recovered, and was chattering about the prairie's beauty, the need for the steel plow to feed the world, the fragility of our

258

environment. "Some plants are so vulnerable—a little less average rainfall, lower winter temperatures, a new animal for which it's food—blam! Gone from the planet forever."

Ted knew he'd passed by something important—not the forgotten bird or flower of West Texas but the soldier by the side of the road. He would have to do more than wave the next time. And he'd explain to others what had to be done.

# About the Author

**Michael Lund** grew up in Rolla, Missouri, holds a PhD in literature from Emory University, and is Professor Emeritus of English at Longwood University in Virginia. He is the author of the Route 66 Novel Series, including *Growing Up on Route 66* (1999); *Route 66 to Vietnam: A Draftee's Story* (2004), and eight other novels about Route 66, all published by BeachHouse Books. Michael served in the U.S. Army, 1969-1971. For more information about Michael's other books, visit http://route66book.com/

Printed in Great Britain
by Amazon

82496912R00153